Truman Lewis Stone

Book II. of the Family of John Stone

one of the first settlers of Guilford, Conn. - also names of all the descendants of

Russell, Bille, Timothy and Eber Stone

Truman Lewis Stone

Book II. of the Family of John Stone
one of the first settlers of Guilford, Conn. - also names of all the descendants of Russell, Bille, Timothy and Eber Stone

ISBN/EAN: 9783337343675

Printed in Europe, USA, Canada, Australia, Japan

Cover: Foto ©Andreas Hilbeck / pixelio.de

More available books at **www.hansebooks.com**

HUMANI
NIHIL
ALIENUM

THE OLD HOMESTEAD

OLD STONE HOUSE.

BOOK II.

OF

The Family of John Stone

ONE OF THE

FIRST SETTLERS OF GUILFORD, CONN.

ALSO

Names of all the Descendents of Russell, Bille, Timothy
and Eber Stone.

BY

TRUMAN LEWIS STONE.

1639

*"A stubborn race, fearing and flattering none,
such are they nurtured, such they live and die."*
—Halleck.

1897

BUFFALO, N. Y.
CHARLES WELLS MOULTON
1898

To The Memory

Of my Father and Mother,

Harvey and Eliza (Lewis) Stone,

This Work is Affectionately

Dedicated by their Son

The Author.

PREFACE.

IN 1890 my uncle, S. D. Lewis of Warsaw, N. Y.,
prepared and published a genealogy of my mother's
family, entitled "Book XVIII Lewis Family Genealogy." From reading that book, I discovered that I
knew very little about my own family ancestry, and as
my mother was alive at that time, I commenced making inquiries of her and my aunt, Lois (Stone) Tilton,
they being the oldest persons then alive in our family.
I found that they knew very little in regard to the
family history. I determined then that I would give
the matter what study I could (which has been at odd
times and evenings, as I am a busy man with very little time that I can call my own). However, the study
instead of being an irksome task, has proven to be a
pleasant pastime. And while I had no idea at first of
publishing the work in book form, from being urged
by friends and relatives of the family who offered to
contribute towards the expense, I have done so.

In preparing this genealogy for the family (as it is
of very little interest to any one not a member of the
family), I have entered upon the task with a sincere
desire to avoid doing injustice to any one, whether a
member of the family or otherwise.

There must be many errors in a work of this kind,
but when I have received dates of births, deaths, etc.,
of the same family by different persons, and they have
disagreed, I have written some member of the family
to correct them. So if you find errors, do not charge

them all to me or the publisher, as I have had to rely entirely on the written data sent me by you.

There are many members of the family who are not alluded to any further than to give date of birth, marriage and death, and who I am confident deserve special mention.

I would have more hope of satisfying the family, if I could have allowed myself more time. I have used my best efforts, with the aid of numerous persons to verify from the records every statement of fact given.

The matter for the biographies has been furnished me by members of the family, which in some instances have taken considerable travel and work to procure; in writing the biographical sketches, there has been no effort made at coloring, but to give a brief sketch that would enable the reader to form a correct idea of the individual; neither has there been any effort made to connect the family by side-lines or otherwise to families that are eminently wealthy or have gained high positions in any of the walks of life; but to give a simple statement of facts, such as dates of birth, marriage and death, with a short biography of each head of the family.

In a great many instances our family can be connected with the families of noted men, such as: Adams, Webster, Thomas Hooker, Grant, Arthur and a host of others. So, also, can any New England family of the Puritan stock connect itself by side lines to these families, or any other families that came to New England in an early day.

A life of peace and prosperity furnishes but little matter for a chronicle. Such, with few exceptions, have been the lives of our family.

This work has been prepared solely for the Stone family and its descendants; and if a stranger or person not a member of the family, should chance to peruse its pages, we trust you will not criticise it although you may be amused at the simplicity of the lives of some of its members. Remember that you are reading a family record that is sacred to some one.

In preparing this work for publication, I have received valuable assistance from a great many members of the family who have furnished me the data from which the genealogy has been prepared; to all of whom I here return my thanks.

My thanks are also due to many gentlemen who have facilitated the collection of material, for the biographies; and especially to Col. Wm. L. Stone of Mt. Vernon, N. Y., who has kindly and freely given me the use of his "Genealogy of The Stone Family," from which the second and third chapter of this work are almost entirely taken. I would also state that this book is the same size of type and page (printed matter) as Col. Stone's Genealogy. I have therefore entitled this volume "Book II of The Family of John Stone, one of the first settlers of Guilford, Conn."

The historical events briefly related in Chapter I, are so closely identified with the early history of our family, that I deemed it essential to concisely relate an account of the most important occurrences of this region. I gladly refer the interested reader to "Smith's History of Guilford" for a more extended account, as it is to this work I am indebted for most of the data for the first chapter. I am also indebted to Wm. Leete Stone, Judge Post, Wm. G. Andrews, D. D., of Guilford, Conn., and others for valuable information to whom I desire to express my thanks.

Finally, I would call attention to the fact that this book contains the names of all the descendants of Russell, Bille, Timothy and Eber down to 1896.

Edward Burk has well said: "Those who do not cherish the memory of their ancestors, do not deserve to be remembered by posterity."

Varysburg, N. Y., Sept. 1, 1897.

TRUMAN LEWIS STONE.

P. S.

Since writing the above, the genealogy has met with hard luck; after most of the book was published and in readiness for the binder, fire broke out in the building in which the work was being done, and destroyed not only the printed matter but most of MS. However, with what was saved from the fire, together with proof sheets and memoranda that I had at my command, I have been enabled to reproduce the book in some respects in better form than the first copy.

The fates seem to have been against the little book since it got into the printers' hands, as the delays have been many and of long duration.

T. L. S.

DESCRIPTION OF COAT-OF-ARMS.

In the Church of St. Mary de Holm-by-the-Sea against the east pillar of the Nave, a mural monument stands bearing the effigies of a man and his wife; behind him are seven sons, and behind her six daughters, all kneeling with the Arms of Stone-Argent. These are three Cinque-foils sable, a chief Azure, impalingbarry of six argent and sable, a band over all azure.

The epitaph, translated from the original Latin is as follows: "Here underneath lyeth Richard Stone and Clemens his wife, who lyved in wedlock joyfully together 64 years and 3 months. From them proceeded 7 sons and 6 daughters: and from them and theirs issued 72 children, which the sayde Richard and Clemens to their great comfort did behold."

LIST OF PORTRAITS AND VIEWS.

THE GUILFORD GREEN.

GENEALOGY OF THE STONE FAMILY

GUILFORD.

Chapter I.

Guilford is a village of about three thousand inhabitants, located on Long Island Sound, about twenty miles east of New Haven, in the State of Connecticut.

It was settled in 1639 by a company of Puritans from Surrey, and Kent County, England, under the leadership of the Rev. Henry Whitfield. The original town included the present towns of Madison and Guilford, stretched along the shore of Long Island Sound, from Branford to Killingworth, a distance on a straight line of nine or ten miles, and extending back from the Sound about the same distance; the whole original town, like others in the vicinity and country, was originally inhabited by Indians, who called it, or at least the western part of it, Menunka-tuck; they were numerous on the great plain south of Guilford borough, as appears from the vast amount of shells brought upon it, and which are mouldering there to this day.

The part of the township, which embraces nearly

MEMORANDA.

all of the present town of Guilford, was purchased of the sachem-squaw of Menunkatuck, Shaumpishuh [the Indian inhabitants consenting] September 29, 1639, by Henry Whitfield, Robert Kitchell, William Leete (afterwards Governor Leete) William Chittenden, John Bishop and John Caffinge, in behalf of themselves and others who had come out to New Haven the same year and who were now resolved to make a settlement at this place. At the time of the purchase it was understood and agreed that the deed should remain in the hands of the planters until a church should be organized in the town, to whom it should be given, and under whose superintendence the lands should be divided out, to those who were interested in them. The articles given for this tract were twelve coats, twelve fathoms of wampum, twelve glasses, twelve pairs of shoes, twelve hatchets, twelve pairs of stockings, twelve hoes, four kettles, twelve knives, twelve hats, twelve porringers, twelve spoons, and two English coats.

The English settlement commenced immediately after this purchase, on the grounds now included in Guilford borough, the plain, and some lands near the Sound, having been cleared by the Indians, and prepared for cultivation.

Mr. Whitfield was desirous of extending the plantation (as they called it) and it was through him that other purchases of land were made from the Indians, a part of which was purchased from Uncas, who probably claimed the land in virtue of the conquest of the Pequoids, in which he assisted.

The first settlers of this town came from Surrey and Kent, near London, England, and were mostly farmers. They had not a merchant among them and scarcely a mechanic. so it was at great trouble and

MEMORANDA.

expense that they procured a blacksmith on their plantation.

They called the town Guilford in remembrance of *Guilford*, a borough town, the capital of Surrey, where many of them had lived.

About forty planters came into the town in 1639. There were forty-eight in 1650, which undoubtedly included the original forty.

The Rev. Henry Whitfield, William Leete, *John Stone*, John's brother, William, and at least twenty-one others, some with families, others with none; set sail from London, England, on May 20th, 1639, for the New World. They styled themselves the Guilford Company, and on the first day of June, 1639, while on shipboard, the little band signed a plantation covenant in which they expressed a purpose to settle near Quinnipiack (New Haven). The covenant signed reads as follows:

COVENANT.

We, whose names are hereunder written, intending by God's gracious permission to plant ourselves in New England, and, if it may be, in the southerly part, about Quinnipiack: We do faithfully promise each to each for ourselves and families and those that belong to us; that we will, the Lord assisting us, sit down and join ourselves together in one intire plantation; and to be helpful each to the other in every common work, according to every man's ability and as need shall require; and we promise not to desert or leave each other or the plantation, but with the consent of the rest, or the greater part of the company who have entered into this engagement.

As for our gathering together in a church way, and the choice of officers and members to be joined

MEMORANDA.

together in that way, we do refer ourselves until such time as it shall please God to settle us in our plantation.

In witness whereof we subscribe our hauds, the first day of June, 1639.

Robert Kitchell,	*John Stone*,
Thomas Norton,	John Bishop,
William Plane,	Abraham Cruttenden.
Francis Bushnell,	Richard Gutridge.
Francis Chatfield,	William Chittenden.
John Hughes,	William Halle,
William Leete,	Wm. Dudley.
Thomas Naish,	Thomas Joanes,
John Parmelin,	Henry Kingsnorth.
John Jurdon,	John Mepham,
Henry Doude,	*William Stone*,
Henry Whitfield,	Thomas Cooke.

John Hoadly.

Between the 10th and 15th of July, 1639, they entered New Haven harbor, their ships (for they had two), being the first vessels that had entered it. After landing at New Haven measures were immediately taken to find a suitable location for the Company, and after careful examination they soon decided upon "Menunkatuck," to which they subsequently gave the name of Guilford, and before winter, had built their houses and moved into them, among which was the noted stone house of Henry Whitfield, which is said to be the oldest house in Connecticut. It was built in 1639. "Palfrey's History of New England" says, "it was erected both for the accommodation of his family, and as a fortification, for the protection of the inhabitants against the Indians." This house was kept in this original form until 1868 when it underwent such

MEMORANDA.

renovation as changed its appearance and internal arrangements to a great extent, although the north wall and large stone chimney are substantially the same as they have been for over two-hundred-fifty years. The walls are of stone from a ledge eighty rods distant to the east, and were probably brought on hand-barrows across a swamp, over a rude causeway which is still to be traced; a small addition has been made to the back of the house in modern times, but there is no question that the main building remains in its original state, even to the oak of the beams, floors, doors, and window frames. The height of the first story is seven feet, and eight inches, the second story, six feet nine inches. The house occupies a rising ground overlooking the great plain south of the village, and commanding a very fine prospect of the Sound. It is said the first marriage was celebrated in it—the wedding table being garnished with the substantial luxuries of pork and peas. This house, and the farm in connection with it is now owned by Mrs. S. B. Cone of Stockbridge.

On the opposite side of the street (Whitfield Street) and nearer the village green, was the allotment of *John Stone.* How long he owned this place is uncertain but Rev. Joseph Eliot purchased the place in 1664, and his descendants own the place to this day, except a lot that was sold off and was the home of the late Dr. Talcott. The places where most of the original settlers located themselves are now known. The road through Guilford was, before railroads, much used by travelers from New York and Boston. The N. Y. N. H. & H. Shore line now runs trains through this place to New York and Boston almost every hour. The first society was famous for raising corn, it was said as much as a *hundred* bushels of ears

MEMORANDA.

had been raised on an acre, but that forty bushels was a fair yield.

Menunkatuck or West River, which runs by the place of *Caleb Stone* (now owned by his descendant *William Leete Stone*) rises in Quonepaug pond, in North Guilford, and empties into Guilford harbor.

Thomas Chittenden, the first Governor of Vermont, was a native of this town. Fitz-Green Halleck, the poet, was born in Guilford, he was the first American poet to whom was awarded the honor of a bronze statue in a public place. It occupies a prominent position in Central Park, New York.

George Hill, the poet, was born in Guilford.

> "Meanwhile a younger race, a different age,
>   Has risen up to occupy the stage,
>   Yet oft I think of Guilford, with delight,
>   And feel full half way there, while this I write."
>   —*Halleck.*

The people of Guilford in September, 1889, held a celebration commemorating the establishment in 1639 of the plantation of Menunkatuck (now represented by the towns of Guilford and Madison), it being the two-hundreth-fiftieth anniversary. The exercises Sunday, September 8th, consisted of sermons preached in the churches of Guilford and Madison (once East Guilford). At 2:30 p. m., Rev. C. L. Kitchell of New Haven, Conn., "who is a descendant of Robert Kitchell, 1639," preached a historical sermon in the First Congregational Church at Guilford from which the following is an extract:

MEMORANDA.

FROM A HISTORICAL SERMON.

—BY—

REV. CORNELIUS L. KITCHELL OF NEW HAVEN.

By faith Abraham, when he was called, obeyed to go out into a place which he was to receive for an inheritance: and he went out not knowing whither he went.—HEBREWS xi: 8.

Just how the call came to Abraham we do not know. But while he was living in Ur of the Chaldees, God, in some way, spake to him, and said: "Get thee out from thy country and from thy kindred and from thy father's house unto a land that I will show thee."

To this divine mandate Abraham was not disobedient. The home of his childhood, the home of his fathers was dear to him, but there he could not worship as he would the one holy and living God. Far to the west, across the deserts, was a land where, unmolested, he and his children could follow the dictates of their finer spiritual instinct. The thought of that country whispered to his soul in divine accents. It would not let him rest. God called him. A divine promise, large and sure, beckoned him. And so, with a chosen company, he set out not knowing whither he went, knowing only that the God who called him would lead him and give him an inheritance in the land of promise.

Since Abraham's day many children of his, in spirit, have heard a like call and have left their homes with a like faith, but, of them all, none were truer descendants of the Father of the Faithful than the

MEMORANDA.

little company whose history we are to trace today. Two hundred and fifty years ago our ancestors who settled this town were living, most of them, in Surrey and Kent, those southern counties which are called, for their richness and beauty, the garden of England. It was a time of ease and of peace in temporal things. They were comfortably provided with this world's goods for their station, surrounded with relatives and friends, proud and fond of England, their native land; but a tyrannical king and a bigoted prelate forced upon them the superstitious observances, as it seemed to them, of that Roman church from which they had hoped they were free. They could not conscientiously conform thereto. If they did not, fines, persecutions, imprisonments, exiles, were inflicted upon them. They heard of a New England across the sea, where others who sympathized with them had fled and found, as yet, freedom to worship God. Just as surely as Canaan was a land of promise to Abraham, New England was to our forefathers. God said to them just as clearly as he did to the ancient patriarch: "Get thee out from your country and from your kindred and from your father's house." By faith, obeying that call, they went out, a little company, bidding good-bye to friends and native land, in frail and diminutive vessels, across the perilous sea, into the uncultivated wilderness, destitute of habitation, haunted by savages, out beyond the older settlements, that without peradventure they might be beyond the reach of the tyrant's arm, and there in the wisdom of the Scriptures and of common sense, in the fear of God, they laid unique foundations of a free Commonwealth and a free Church, from which, and others like them, as the centuries rolled on has developed the great nation in which we dwell. The land to which they were

MEMORANDA.

called they did afterward inherit. The text thus suggests the two-fold aspect, namely, the Going out in Faith and the Inheriting the Land, under which we may include the origin and the development of the Church of Christ here.

FIRST: GOING OUT IN FAITH.

Sometime in September, 1639 (O. S.), certain planters of this colony, seeking a habitation, came to Menunkatuck, as the region was called. Pleased with what they found, on the 29th of September, articles of agreement were signed by six of them representing the whole colony, and the sachem-squaw who claimed ownership. In consideration of sundry coats, fathoms of wampum, glasses, shoes, hatchets, etc., "the said sachem-squaw did sell to the aforesaid English planters all the land within the limits of Ruttawoo (East River) and Agicomick river (Stony Creek)," the present limits of Guilford. Immediately after this purchase, before winter probably, the whole company came over from New Haven where they had disembarked the June preceding, and took possession of lands near the Sound, "especially the great plain south of the town," which the historian tells us had been "already cleared and enriched by the natives." While the little community is getting itself into shape, let us ask who they are and how they have been led here.

First of all, we need to note that they are but a little band of a vast company. It has been computed that between the years 1630 and 1640 more than 20,000 persons arrived in New England from the mother country. It was the time of Charles the first and his Archbishop Laud, the time of the Star Chamber and High Commissions. Many of the most active and

MEMORANDA.

most Godly ministers of the Church of England with their congregations, though they loved their "dear mother Church," as they did not cease to call her, could not conform to the superstitious ceremonies arbitrarily prescribed, and as non-conformists, fled to New England.

One such minister was Henry Whitfield, of Ockley in Surrey, who became the leader and pastor of the company which settled in Guilford. Cotton Mather, in his Magnalia, tells of him that he was educated to be a lawyer, "first at the University and then at the Inns of Court. But the gracious and early operation of the Holy Spirit on his heart inclined him rather to be a preacher of the Gospel." For twenty years he was a conformist, but as the result of an interview with Rev. John Cotton (afterward pastor at Boston) and Rev. John Davenport (afterward pastor at New Haven) both of whom for their non-conformity were later compelled to fly, first to Holland and thence to New England, "Whitfield embraced a modest secession," as Cotton Mather phrases it. Summoned once and again before the archbishop's court, and becoming liable to censure, no longer able "to proceed in the public exercise of his ministry," he resigned his rich living, sold his personal estate and became the leader of these Surrey and Kent farmers. They knew his piety and his ability from missionary work he had done among them, and "felt they could not do without his ministry." Like him, too, they considered affairs at home were hopeless, and duty called them to lay new foundations for Christ's kingdom beyond the sea.

Two other men of this little colony we need to note. One of them, William Leete, was afterward magistrate here in Guilford, then Governor of New Haven Colony, later deputy Governor of the United

MEMORANDA.

Colony of Connecticut, and later still for several years
Governor of Connecticut, by annual election till he
died.   The decided and excellent quality of this man
appeared early.   He is the only member of this little
colony except Mr. Whitfield whose experience in England, Cotton Mather tells us of.

The other notable person was Samuel Desborough,
whose brother married the sister of Oliver Cromwell,
and who in later years under the Lord Protector was
Keeper of the Great Seal of Scotland, training for
which high office he had in being one of the seven
pillars of the church and magistrate here in Guilford,
before yet he returned to England.

Around these men as leaders gathered the sturdy
farmers of Kent and Surrey, young men, most of
them, we are told, forty planters in all, and embark-
ing from London in May, 1639, in two vessels probably, began their long voyage of forty-nine days across
the Atlantic.

Now in regard to this company, note that while
they were not organized as a church, yet they were
distinctively a religious community, whose leader
was their pastor and whose "Design was Religion."
Their main object was not adventure, nor trade, nor
the improvement of their personal estates.   They
were indeed of that great race in whose blood has
ever been a readiness to brave danger, and I do not
deny that they were sagacious and thrifty men bound
to do as best they could for their families and estates,
but first of all they did seek the Kingdom of God and
His righteousness.   Listen to what they declare four
years later when they were about to form their civil
government: "The mayne ends which were pro-
pounded to ourselves in our coming hither and settling
down together are. that we may settle and uphold the

MEMORANDA.

ordinances of God in an explicit Congregational Church way with most purity, peace liberty for the benefit both of ourselves and posterity after us."

They landed at New Haven probably toward the end of June. Sometime before the 29th of September, they held their first meeting of which we have any record, in Mr. Newman's barn in New Haven, and agreed that the lands called Menunkatuck should be purchased for them and their heirs, "the deed-writings there about to be made and drawn in the name of these six planters in our steads, viz.: Henry Whitfield, Robert Kitchell, William Leete, William Chittenden, John Bishop, and John Caffinge."

These six planters as directed, purchased the land, and the little colony of about two hundred souls we may suppose, as has been before narrated, came over from New Haven before winter and the history of this community began.

And now for nearly four years, until June 19th, 1643, when the church was first formally instituted, but little is recorded. That they nourished a vigorous religious and devotional life in all this period of patient waiting, as we should otherwise suppose is indicated also by the fact that midway in it, in 1641, the Rev. John Higginson was called as "teacher" to assist Mr. Whitfield, the pastor, in his work. Why they did not organize a church at once, we can only conjecture. Most likely they felt less need of such organization, because they were, as it were, a church already. Not only was Mr. Whitfield, their leader, a regular clergyman whose ordination they accepted and never had repeated (as was done in the case of Mr. Davenport at New Haven and others), but many of them had enjoyed his ministrations in their former homes, and

MEMORANDA.

one of them, Mr. Thomas Norton, had been warden of Mr. Whitfield's church at Ockley.

That they kept the formation of a church steadily in view is evident from this record of an agreement made at a meeting of the planters held February 2d, 1642, at a time when the need of some more explicit kind of civil government appears first to have found expression: "It is agreed that the civil power of administration of justice and preservation of peace shall remain in the hands of Robert Kitchel, William Chittenden, John Bishop and William Leete, formerly chosen for that work, until some may be chosen *out of the church that shall be gathered here.*"

How long this inderminate condition of Church and State would have continued, had not some impulse come from without, it would be difficult to say. Such an impulse, however, did come in the spring of 1643, at which time it became necessary, owing to the breach then existing between King and Parliament, for the colony here to combine with New Haven and the other New England colonies for the sake of security. But in order to do this, it was necessary that Guilford should adopt some definite civil constitution and form of government, and as in their idea, the civil government was to be the creature of the church, the church itself must be first definitely organized that it might, in turn, call the civil body into existence.

Accordingly on June 19th, 1643, the first step was taken by choosing seven men to be the "seven pillars." These seven pillars were the pastor, Henry Whitfield, his assistant and son-in-law John Higginson, Samuel Desborough, William Leete, Jacob Sheaffe, John Mipham and John Hoadley. This was in accordance with the method pursued in New Haven four years before, at the suggestion of Rev. John Daven-

MEMORANDA.

port, the pastor there, who derived this method of ecclesiastical organization from the text: "Wisdom hath builded her house, she hath hewn out her seven pillars." This may seem to us rather heroic homiletis, but practically at that time it met the case. These Christians in the wilderness had cut loose from the ancient foundations. They were feeling for the simplicity of the early Church which gathered about Christ as the only foundation, and practically they attained it. Yet, members as they were of the ancient Church of England, it must have satisfied their imagination and filled a void in their hearts, *to have something to join.* These seven godly, Christian men, choicest of the whole band—these seven pillars in some unconscious way and with a sort of Scriptural sanction stood to them, we cannot doubt, in place of the goodly battlements of that great historic Church from which they never separated, but from which they were now cutting loose.

These seven elect men first drew up a "Doctrine of Faith," the same used in the First Church, till in 1837 it was somewhat amended. To this they formally assented and then entered into covenant with God and each other. Thus was laid the foundation. Then the other members joined themselves to these seven pillars by making the same profession and covenant and the church was fully gathered and established.

Of the newly organized church Mr. Whitfield continued to be pastor just as he had been of the colony from the beginning. It would seem that he was never formally chosen pastor by the church nor installed, probably because for several years he had actually been their pastor and in the work and was a regularly ordained clergyman.

MEMORANDA.

Rev. John Higginson was also continued as "teacher." He preached one-half day every Sabbath and had charge of the public school. The office of ruling elder, which existed in New Haven and other New England churches was not adopted here. Neither were deacons chosen either in Mr. Whitfield's or Mr. Higginson's ministry, that is, for nearly a quarter of a century. Three men were chosen annually who collected the minister's maintenance, and managed the temporalities of the church like vestrymen in the Church of England. To the church thus constituted the four planters who had been entrusted with the control of affairs until a church should be gathered, resigned their trust and by the church thus organized the civil polity of the plantation was thereupon established.

In that civil polity the feature which now seems most peculiar, and for which the church is justly held responsible, is the provision that only church members should be voting citzens. This is fully expressed in the constitution which the church drafted for the civil government now to be set up by it. It reads: "We do now therefore all and every of us agree, order and conclude that only such planters as are also members of the church here shall be and be called freemen and that such freemen only shall have power to elect magistrates, deputies and other officers of public interest, or authoriy in matters of importance, concerning either the civil affairs or government here, from amongst themselves and not elsewhere." In a word, only church members could vote or be voted for.

What our fathers thus did was with entire unanimity, in accordance with the high purpose that actuated them, to erect a miniature republic in which the good should rule. They thought they had found who

MEMORANDA.

the good were, namely, those who by a regenerating faith had become members of the true Church of Christ. So they established a popular government with a "piety qualification"—not property nor learning but personal character should be the test of citizenship.

That such were the motives that induced our fathers to thus limit citizenship appears very clearly in a treatise written at that time, probably by Rev. John Davenport (though ascribed on its title page to John Cotton), entitled "A Discourse about Civil Government in a New Plantation whose Design is Religion." In this note the Sixth Argument, (which doubtless underlay all the rest) namely: "The danger of devolving this (civil) power upon those not in church order." When Mr. Davenport came to the Massachusetts colony on his way to New Haven, he found that they in Massachusetts had seven years before (May 18th, 1631) limited citizenship in the same way. They had done so in part because they were afraid that otherwise emissaries of the King, or of Laud, might gain entrance into their councils. The same danger existed here and they sought to escape it in the same way.

MEMORANDA.

CHAPTER II.

REV. SAMUEL STONE.

"'And who were they, our fathers?' In their veins
  Ran the best blood of England's gentlemen;
Her bravest in the strife on battle plains,
  Her wisest in the strife of voice and pen;
Her holiest, teaching, in her holiest fanes,
  The lore that led to martyrdom; and when
On this side ocean slept their wearied sails,
And their toil-bells woke up our thousand hills and dales,

'Shamed they their fathers?' Ask the village spires
  Above their Sabbath homes of praise and prayer:
Ask of their children's happy household fires,
  And happier harvest noons; ask summer's air,
Made merry by young voices, when the wires
  Of their school cages are unloosed."

—Halleck's Connecticut.

(1)

I. REV. SAMUEL STONE, a non-conformist divine of Hereford, Hereforshire, on the Wye south of London, in Surrey County, England, was undoubtedly our English ancestor. Although there is a difference in opinion on that subject, Col. William L. Stone of Mt. Vernon, N. Y., who has written a book entitled "The Family of John Stone," seems to have no doubt but that the Rev. Samuel Stone was our English ancestor. He says in the introductory of his work: "Various have been the traditions concerning the origin of the Stone family in America. The most commonly accepted one has been that six brothers came over in a vessel of their own to Watertown, Mass.; that their names respectively were: Deacon Simon, (others say Rev. Simon) Stone, William Stone, John Stone, Deacon Gregory Stone, Isaac Stone, and

"

MEMORANDA.

Rev. Samuel Stone. That the first three settled at Watertown (some say little Cambridge and Dorchester), William and John at Guilford, Conn., and Rev. Samuel at Hartford, Conn." This tradition further states that they were all the sons of Rev. Samuel Stone, a non-conformist divine of Herefordshire, England, and educated at Emanuel College, Cambridge, and a lecturer in Torcester, Northamptonshire (*From Cotton Mathers Magnolia, Vol. 1, P. 392-5, Hartford, 1820.*) On the other hand and in direct conflict with above "A History of the first church in Hartford, Conn., states that Rev. Samuel Stone was a son of John Stone, a freeholder of Herford, England. This is based on investigations made in England, on the records of Hertford, and so far as the ancestry of Rev. Samuel (who founded Hartford, Conn.) is concerned, this statement is undoubtedly the correct one; (in regard to the history of Rev. Samuel Stone, who was the founder of Hartford, more can be found in a work printed by George Leon Walker in 1884; in the course of his story of the old first church of Hartford, he has a good deal to say of Rev. Samuel Stone). The register of the "Church of All Saints," Hertford (not Hereford,) Eng., has the following entries of the baptisms of Rev. Samuel Stone of Hartford (not Rev. Samuel of England) and his brothers and sisters:

Jeremyas, son of John Stone, baptized February 18, 1599.

Samuel, son of John Stone, baptized July 30, 1602.

Jerome, son of John Stone, baptized September 29, 1604.

John, son of John Stone, baptized July 6, 1607.

Mary, daughter of John Stone, baptized January 13, 1609.

MEMORANDA.

Ezechiel, son of John Stone, baptized November 1, 1612.

Lidda, daughter of John Stone, baptized April 17, 1616.

Elizabeth, daughter of John Stone, baptized October 21, 1621.

Sara, daughter of John Stone, baptized April 3, 1625.

Ezechiel, son of John Stone, baptized April 27, 1629.

Jeremy, buried January 19, 1601.

John, buried October 8, 1609.

Ezechiel, buried April 27, 1629.

Lidda, buried August 10, 1635.

This record seems to explode the tradition of the "Six Brothers" for Rev. Samuel, "of Hartford," was the son of *John*, not of *Samuel*, and Simon, and Gregory could hardly have been his brothers, even supposing that their baptisms do not appear on the Hertford register was from neglect to record them or from some other cause, since it is known (from their ages) that Simon was born in 1585, and Gregory in 1590. It is therefore extremely unlikely that they were the brothers of Samuel, whose father continued to have children as late as 1629.

It has also been stated that Simon Stone "came over from Ipswich in the ship Increase April 15th, 1635." Of John Stone, Col. William L. Stone says that he has come across no less than ten of that name who were early settlers in New England. A Stone Genealogy of the Rhode Island branch, says that a John Stone, aged forty, came to Salem, Mass., in April, 1635, from Hawkhurst, England, in the ship Elizabeth, where he remained for some years plying a ferry between that village and Beverly, finally moving to Guilford, Conn.

MEMORANDA.

MEMORANDA.

A Hugh Stone, also, settled in Cranston, R. I., and was the founder of the Stones in that State.

It would appear from the foregoing that it is useless to try to trace the Stone family in America, from a single source. There were doubtless many of that name who were among the earliest emigrants to the colonies, and who, in all probability, were in nowise related to each other. Fortunately, however, for us, no such obscurity envelops our New England ancestor, and while it might have been pleasant to believe that we were directly descended from Rev. Samuel Stone, the founder of Hartford, and the faithful companion and friend of the devoted Hooker, yet the contrary finds more than its compensation in the certainty with which patient investigation has answered the question, who was our American Ancestor? Who the parents were of Rev. Samuel Stone, "our English Ancestor," cannot be ascertained from the fact that he was a non-conformist divine, consequently no records of his marriage and ancestors exist in Parish records. Had he been of the Church of England no such difficulty would have existed.

MEMORANDA.

SECOND GENERATION.

Chapter III.

Children of the Rev. Samuel Stone of Hereford, England.

(2)

I. JOHN STONE, the founder of our house in America, was the son of Rev. Samuel Stone, a nonconformist divine, of Hereford, on the Wye of Herefordshire, England. He was born in Herefordshire near Guilford (probably at Okley) the borough town of Surrey County, about 1610, and came to New England in the summer of 1639 in company of William Leete (afterward Governor Leete) and Rev. Henry Whitfield, settling in what is now called Guilford, Connecticut. John and his brother William came in Whitfield's first Guilford company, having set sail from England, May 20, 1639, in two ships. When their ships had been about ten days out these brothers, with William Leete and others, of their companions, entered into a written agreement, or as it was called, a "Plantation Covenant." (See page 5.) Between the 10th and 15th of July their ships dropped anchor in the harbor at New Haven, the first vessels that had ever entered it. John was a farmer, also by trade a clothier, and a mason. It being no uncommon thing in those days for a man to have two, or even more trades. He was for many years town constable, an office which was far more respectable than that of sheriff is now. He seems to have been a man well

MEMORANDA.

thought of among his fellows, since his family not only intermarried with that of Governor Leete, but he was often employed by the Selectmen of the town, as Referee, in varicus cases in which high character and strict probity were required. John's first allotment of land was on what is now Whitfield Street, opposite Henry Whitfield's first place, and near the village green. How long he owned this place is not known, but Rev. Joseph Eliott purchased the place in 1664 and his descendants own the place to this day. One that is competent to know says that John Stone's place was afterward at the corner of York and Fair streets, the present site of the Institute, or high school.

John's brother William* was the ancestor of (Lois Stone* 30) who married (Russell Stone* 30). William was a farmer and kept an inn at North Guilford. He came to Guilford with his wife Hannah with the fisrt company. He married for a second wife in 1659. Mary Hughes, and died November, 1683.

John Stone married in 1642, Mary ——, and died at Guilford February, 1687.

*For Genealogy of William's family, see Appendix.

MEMORANDA.

THIRD GENERATION.

Chapter IV.

Children of John (2) and Mary (—) Stone, all born at Guilford, Conn.

(3)

I. JOHN was born August 14, 1644. He married Susannah Newton, a daughter of Roger Newton and Mary Hooker, and granddaughter of Thomas Hooker, an eminent divine, one of the founders of the Congregational Church in America, together with Rev. Samuel Stone, and John Cotton, and founder of Hartford, Connecticut.

JOHN, JR., died at Milford, Conn., one year before his father, viz., 1686. They had three children viz.:

1. Susannah, born 1674, died 1722; no children.

2. John, born 1676, died at Stamford, Conn., December 13, 1723.

3. Ezekiel, born 1678, married (———).

(4)

II. SAMUEL, born December 6, 1646, married November 1, 1683, Sarah Taintor, born October, 1658, a daughter of Michael Taintor, of Branford, Conn. Samuel died at Guilford, April 5, 1708; Sarah died at Guilford, July —, 1732. They had eight children, viz.:

1. Sarah, born September 22, 1684, died September 22, 1684.

MEMORANDA.

2. Samuel, born April 25, 1685, married Mercey Rowlee.

3. Abigail, born January 31, 1687, died October 10, 1703.

4. Sarah, born May 26, 1689, married Bezaleel Bristol.

5. Deborah, born May 26, 1689, married Thomas Ward.

6. Mary, born August 13, 1692, married Hugh White.

7. Bathsheba, born August 10, 1695, married Timothy Baldwin.

8. Elizabeth, born October 1, 1697, married Abraham Bradley.

(5)

III. Nathaniel was born September 15, 1648. He married, July 10, 1673, Mary Bartlett, daughter of George Bartlett and Mary Crittenden or "Cruttenden" of Guilford. He seems to have been a man of some importance in the Colony, since we find him a lieutenant in the militia in 1702, and also the same year a deputy to the first and second sessions of the General Court at New Haven. He died August 11, 1709. His widow, born February 1, 1654, survived him several years, dying November 5, 1724.

(6)

IV. THOMAS was born June 5, 1650. He married, December 13, 1676, Mary Johnson, who was born February 21, 1657. She was a daughter of William Johnson and Elizabeth Bushnell. Thomas died December 1, 1683. Mary, his wife, died July 6, 1732. (There must have been a mistake in the record of the death of Thomas as they are said to have had ten children),

MEMORANDA.

however the names of the only ones that have come
down are:

1. Benjamin, born March 11, 1678, married first
Sarah Minor; second Sarah Dodd.

2. Mary Dorothy, married Ebenezer Ingham.

(7)

V. NOAH, born in 1652, died March 30, 1684.

MEMORANDA.

FOURTH GENERATION.

Chapter V.

Children of Nathaniel (5) and Mary (Bartlett) Stone, all born at Guilford, Conn.

(8)

I. JOSEPH, born June 17, 1674, married Mary Scrantton.

(9)

II. EBENEZER, born August 21, 1676, married first, Hannah Norton, born February 24, 1678, a daughter of John Norton and Hannah Stone of North Guilford. She died March 5, 1723. They had five children, viz.:

1. Anna, born March 8, 1703, died young.

2. Ebenezer, born March 10, 1706, married Sybil Leete.

3. Noah, born October 1, 1711, —— ——.

4. Seth, born August 10, 1714, died October 14, 1715.

5. Seth, born July 12, 1718, married Rachael Leete.

Edenezer married for a second wife in 1725, the widow of Abraham Bradley of Guilford. Her maiden name was Abigail Leete, a daughter of Hon. Andrew Leete, the second son of Governor William Leete. She died April 16, 1767. He had two children by this wife, viz.:

1. Abigail, born October 2, 1726, died November 3, 1783.

MEMORANDA.

2. Mary, born ——, 1728, married —— Caldwell.

Ebenezer died August 18, 1761, at the age of 85 years.

(10)

III. NATHANIEL was born October 7, 1678, married January 6, 1709, Hannah Graves. They had five cildren, viz.:
1. Hannah.
2. Nathaniel.
3. Hulda.
4. Elizabeth.
5. Thomas.

(11)

IV. ANNA, born January 29, 1681, died November 6, 1684.

(12)

V. CALEB, born April 26, 1683, died March, 1684.

(13)

VI. CALEB was born November 10, 1685, and died May 25, 1765. He married, May 28, 1713, Sarah Meigs, who was born at East Guilford in 1690, and died May 4, 1775. He was a daughter of deacon John Meigs of East Guilford. He was born November 11, 1670, was the first magistrate at East Guilford, and took an active part in all the Indian troubles. Her brother, Junna was grandfather of the famous Col. Return Jonathan Meigs, born December 17, 1740. He was Colonel of the 6th Connecticut line, in the Revolution, was at Quebec under Arnold, holding the rank of Major, was there taken prisoner. He was at Sag-

MEMORANDA.

Harbor and Stony Point.   He settled at Marietta, Ohio, in 1788.   His son, Return Jonathan, Jr., was Chief Justice of the Supreme Court of Ohio, in 1803-4, Colonel in the United States Army 1804-6, a Judge in Louisiana 1805-6, United States District Judge in Michigan 1807-8; he was United States Senator from Ohio, 1808-10; Governor of that State 1810-14, United States Postmaster-General 1814-23.

The year following Caleb's marriage he purchased of John Leete, a grandson of Governor William Leete, the east half of Governor Leete's allotment, containing two acres and thirty-two rods of land.   The following is a true copy of the original deed, which Miss Anna Stone, a descendant of Caleb, has in a neat frame, which graces her parlor, on this same place:

To all Christian People to whom these presents shall come, John Leete, of Guilford, County of New Haven, and Colony of Connecticut, yeoman sendeth greeting.   Know ye, that I, the said John Leete, for, and in consideration of the full, and just sum of 30 pounds, silver money, had, and received at the hand of Caleb Stone, of the above said Town, County and Colony; yeomen, have, and by these presence do, from me, my heirs, and executors, fully, freely, and absolutely Give, Grant, Alean, Sell, Convey, and Confirm unto the above-named Caleb Stone, his heirs, and assigns forever, one tract or parcel of land, situated in Guilford, above said, it being part of my home lot, bounded northerly by the land of Samuel Johnson, east by the land of John Norton, south on the street or highway, westerly by land of Benjamin Leete, containing two acres, and thirty-two rods, which lands are a part of my inheritance left me by my deceased father, John Leete.   All the said land now to be, Continue, and Abide unto the said Caleb Stone to him, his heirs, and assigns

MEMORANDA

forever, full and clear, together with all, and singular, the privileges and appurtenances, thereunto belonging, or in anywise appertaining, to have, and to hold, possess, and enjoy, the same as a full, clear, and absolute estate in fee simple, full, and clearly acquitted, of and from all, and all manner of former gifts, grants, conveyances, mortgages, or incumbrances of law whatever. Further, I, the said John Leete, bind myself, my heirs, and executors, to warrant, and defend the sale of the above bargained premises unto the above said Caleb Stone, to him, his heirs, and assigns forever.

In witness whereof I have hereunto set my name and affixed my seal this 4th day of July, and in the thirteenth year of the reign of our sovereign Lady Ann, Queen of Great Britain, and in the year of our Lord, one thousand seven hundred and fourteen.

JOHN LEETE. [*Seal.*]

Signed, sealed, and delivered in the presence of

ANDREW WARD,
ANDREW WARD, 2d.

July 20th, 1714, John Leete of Guilford, did acknowledge the above written instrument to be his free act and deed. Before me.   *JAMES HOOKER,*

Justice.

The next year, 1715, he purchased of Benjamin Leete and Rachel Leete, his wife, the balance of Governor Leete's Allotment containing about the same number of acres. Benjamin Leete was also a grandson of Governor Leete. This land lay on the west side of the first purchase made of John Leete at the corner of Broad and River streets, in Guilford: it included Governor Leete's old store, and was conveyed by Benjamin Leete and his wife, Rachel Leete, as property they had inherited. The consideration named is seventy-one pounds. William Leete Stone,

MEMORANDA.

a descendant of Caleb Stone, lives on this place at the present time (1894) and has the original deed in a frame on his parlor wall. It is dated as follows:

Benjamin Leete and Rachel, his wife, have hereunto set our hands, and seals, this 30th day of August, in the second year of the reign of our Sovereign Lord, George, King of Great Britain, and in the year of our Lord, One Thousand, Seven Hundred, Fifteen.

BENJAMIN LEETE. [Seal]
Her
RACHEL + LEETE. [Seal]
Mark.

Signed, Sealed and Delivered
in the Presence of
JOSEPH CRUTTENDEN, {
EBENEZER PARMELEE. }

August 30, 1715, Benjamin Leete, and Rachel Leete, his wife did acknowledge the above written instrument to be their own free act and deed before me.

JAMES HOOKER,
Justice.

The house now standing, and occupied by William Leete Stone, at the corner of Broad and River streets, was built by Caleb Stone in 1749. This property has been in the hands of Caleb Stone and his direct descendants from the time he purchased it till the present, and is now owned and occupied by William Leete Stone, a great-great-great-grandson of Caleb. In this house five generations of the Stone family have been born. The chimney, which is built of stone, measures twelve feet square in the cellar and about four feet square at the top, and has three flues.

MEMORANDA.

This house and property is certainly *the old homestead* of our line of the Stone family.* This place in some respects is the most historical place in Guilford. It was here that William Leete settled in 1639. He was Royal Governor of Connecticut 1661-5 and 1676, until his death at Hartford, April 16, 1683, where he was buried in the old Center Churchyard. It was here that the first white child was born in Guilford, viz.: John Leete, born 1639.

"Styles History of the Judges" says the Governor's house was situated on the east bank of West River. He had a store on the bank a few rods from his house, and under it a cellar, (the walls of which remain to this day, and which the writer visited and viewed with interest May 28, 1894). It is still in the general and concurrent tradition at Guilford, that the Judges Goffe and Whalley were concealed and lodged in this cellar several nights, most say three nights and three days, being constantly supplied with food from the Governor's table. Col. Wm. L. Stone has written an entertaining story called "Mercy Disborough a Tale of the Witches," founded on the fact of Governor Leete's hiding the regicides Goffe and Whalley.

The time of this concealment must have been between June 11 and 20, 1660; here and at Rossiters, they spent above a week. This cellar still remains in good condition and the wall will stand for future generations to inspect. It is now used for the storage of empty barrels.

(14)

VII. NOAH, born November 9, 1687, died June 6, 1703.

---

* See view on another page of this book.

MEMORANDA.

(15)

VIII. JOHN, born October 7, 1689, died young.

(16)

IX. ANNA, born June 17, 1692, married Nathaniel Rossiter.

(17)

X. TIMOTHY, born March 16, 1696, married first Rachel Norton; second. Elizabeth Robinson.

MEMORANDA.

FIFTH GENERATION.

Chapter VI.

(18)

I. CALEB, born May 7, 1714.   Died, July 28, 1788.
He married Rebecca Everts.

(19

II. SARAH, born January 29, 1717.   Died February 17, 1746.   She married Caleb Benton.

(20

III. RHODA, born November 2, 1719.   Married Daniel Leete.   She died December 23, 1769.

(21

IV. DEBORAH, born July 9, 1723.   Died January 10, 1735.

(22)

V. REUBEN, born March 31, 1726, and died at Guilford, Conn., October 5, 1804.   He married first, January 19, 1748, Ann Everts, who was born at Guilford, in 1728, and died August 1, 1763, aged 35 years. He married for a second wife, May 1, 1766, Elizabeth Chittenden (a widow).   She was born July 31, 1731, and died November 10, 1787.

MEMORANDA.

Reuben was born on the place where the old homestead is now standing, at the corner of Broad and River streets. Always living there; he owned the place after his father's death. He built in 1769 a new house on the lot first purchased by his father (Caleb) of John Leete, which is now standing. This house, his son Timothy, in a letter written to his brother, Eber, speaks of as the house built for brother Bille. Reuben was a captain of a company of militia at Guilford. His company turned out at the New Haven Alarm, July 5, 1779—it was Tryson's invasion of Connecticut —his company was under Lieutenant-Colonel Epapheas Sheldon. He was a man well thought of in the community in which he lived as is evidenced by various records of the town.

(23)

VI. SOLOMON was born May 29, 1728, and died June 9, 1729.

(24)

VII. TRYPHENA was born January 16, 1731. She married John Dudley.

MEMORANDA

SIXTH GENERATION.

Chapter VII.

Children of Reuben (22) and Ann (Everts) Stone all born at
Guilford, Conn.

(25)

I. DEBORAH was born October 21, 1748. She
married Ebenezer Bishop.

(26)

II. REUBEN was born May 24, 1750, and died
September 25, 1751.

(27)

III ANNA was born July 17, 1752, and died October 30, 1757.

(28)

IV. RHODA was born December 24, 1754. She
married William Wright. I have been unable to get
any trace of her family.

(29)

V. REUBEN was born November 4, 1756, and
died April 12, 1764.

MEMORANDA.

(30)

VI. RUSSELL was born in the old house now standing at the corner of Broad and River streets, Guilford, Conn., January 26th, 1759. He married in 1780 or 1781 Lois Stone*, a descendant of William Stone, brother of John, the emigrant. Lois was born at Guilford, April 26, 1760, and died March 15, 1831, at Livonia, N. Y. They moved to Hancock, Berkshire County, Mass., some time between 1786 and 1789, and lived there until 1790 or 1791, when they removed with their family to Greenville, Green County, N. Y. He lived there until his death.

Russell was with the Connecticut militia in the Revolution. In November, 1776, the Connecticut Assembly voted to raise four State Battalions to join the Continental Army, then near New York, to serve until March, 1777. These battalions did not march out of the State at that time, but remained in part on the Westchester border under General Wooster, or went to Rhode Island under General Spencer, who was assigned to command in that State in December, 1776. The records are not clear as to the service of these troops.

Russell was in the second battalion of General Gates' army. Thaddeus Cook, Colonel; Epapheas Sheldon, Lieutenant-Colonel; Edward Russell, Major. He was wounded in the hand at Stillwater, September 19, 1777. His wound was not of so serious a nature as to cause him to leave the service,† as he was present

---

* For Genealogy Lois Stone see Appendix.

---

† Russell was wounded in the hand, a thumb or finger shot off, the British ball passed through the stock of the gun, splitting it so that it was wound with a wire for years after. The writer now has the barrel to the old gun.

MEMORANDA.

at the surrender of Burgoyne, October 17, 1777. He died at Greenville, Green County, N. Y., December 11, 1803, and was buried at Norton Hill, Green County, N. Y. A stone marks his resting place upon which is the following inscription:

> "The law of kindness
> Was writen uppon his Heart."

(31)

VII. BILLE was born May 31, 1761. He married, March 22, 1780, Rachel Ward. She was born at Guilford, December 2, 1757, and died at Mount Pleasant, Pa., August 16, 1847. He died at Mount Pleasant, Pa., August 2, 1827. He was a soldier in the Revolution, being a member of the Guilford Guards. He was wounded March 17, 1782.

Children of Reuben (22) and Elizabeth (Chittenden) Stone.

(32)

I. TIMOTHY was born March 4, 1768, and died December 11, 1846. He married, July 19, 1789, Ann Griswold. She was born May 5, 1769, and died December 31, 1846. He owned the old homestead after his father's death. He was elected to the office of magistrate a number of terms.

(33)

II. SARAH was born October 8, 1769, and died July 19, 1842. She never married.

(34)

III. EBER was born September 7, 1773, at Guilford, Conn., and died November 3, 1845, at Westfield,

MEMORANDA.

N. Y. He married at Homer, N. Y., March 12, 1800,
Betsey Atwater, who was born at Hampden, Conn.,
and died at Westfield, N. Y., October 3, 1841. He
moved from Homer, Cortland County, N. Y., to Westfield, N. Y., in February, 1813. Passing through
Buffalo just after the destruction of that place by the
British. There was only one house left in all that city
at that time. His son Lester, now living at Westfield, remembers the occurrence of moving perfectly
well. He was at that time a lad of six years. Eber's
death was caused by a fall from a high bank on Chautauqua Creek, as he was returning from prayer-meet-
ing on a dark night. He was a deacon of the Presbyterian church, and a man highly respected in the community in which he resided.

MEMORANDA.

REUBEN STONE

SEVENTH GENERATION.

Chapter VIII.

(35)

I. JOEL was born at Guilford. Conn., October 26, 1783, and died at Livonia, N. Y., March 13, 1829. Joel married ———— Lucinda Warner, born in Vermont, April 19, 1790. Died at Livonia, N. Y., January 17, 1872. They were undoubtedly married at Greenville, N. Y. He came to Livonia, N. Y.. with his wife and brother Reuben (37) in the winter of 1809-10. He took up a farm that he lived on until his death. He was a man highly esteemed in the community, and was a deacon in the Presbyterian church for many years.

(36)

II. ORIN was born at Guilford. Conn., November 3, 1785. He died at Livonia, N. Y., October 17, 1845. He was married twice, first October 28, 1810, to Clarrissa Cowel, who was born May 31, 1791, and died at Livonia. August 3, 1814. He married for a second wife, February 5, 1815, Betsey Cowel, a sister of his first wife, who was born August 28. 1795. She died at Livonia, May 15, 1842. He was a deacon in the Presbyterian church, and a man well thought of in his community. His occupation was farming.

MEMORANDA.

(37)

III. REUBEN was born at Hancock, Mass., January 26, 1790, and died at Orangeville, Wyoming County, N. Y., April 11, 1869. He was twice married. First, September ——, 1815, to Almira Merrell, a daughter of Noah Merrell, who was a revolutionary soldier, and an early settler in Orangeville. Noah's wife's name was Hepzebah Pettibone. Almira was born at Colebrook, Conn., June 13, 1792, and died at Orangeville, Wyoming County, N. Y., December 22, 1831.

Hepzebah Pettibone was born January 13, 1739. She was a daughter of Isaac Pettibone, born June 19, 1711, and died 1771, and Hepzebah Humphrey who were married February 12, 1738. They removed from Colebrook with Ezekiel Wilcox, to Norfolk, Conn., and lived on the hill about one-half mile east of the meeting house. His widow married Deacon Daniel Morris, and died December 14, 1800, aged 80 years. Isaac was the ancestor of the Pettibone family's of Attica, N. Y.; Isaac was a son of Samuel Pettibone and Judith Shepard, Samuel was born at Simsbury, Conn., September 2, 1672, and died February 11, 1747, he married Judith Shepard in Concord, Mass., they were farmers and lived in Simsbury, Conn.; they were members of the first church in that town.

Samuel was a son of *John Pettibone* and *Sarah Eggleston* who were married at Windsor, Conn., February 16, 1664. One tradition says he was from Wales; he was a farmer, he died July 15, 1713. Sarah Eggleston was a daughter of Begot Eggleston, who first settled at Dorchester, Mass.; she died July 8, 1713; they both died at Simsbury, Conn., where they had resided a great many years; it is said that John

MEMORANDA

MEMORANDA

Pettibone is the ancestor of all the Pettibone family in the United States. Also that his old homestead is still owned by his descendants.

He (Reuben) married the second time, April ——, 1832, Mrs. Julia Dunham, the widow of Simeon Dunham. Julia was a daughter of Seth Porter, born January 2, 1770, and Sarah (Cowls) Porter, born April 10, 1772, and a granddaughter of Captain John Porter, born in 1746, and Jerusha Porter, born December 20, 1747. Julia was born November 30, 1799, and died at Orangeville, N. Y., January 24, 1859. The children of Simeon Dunham and Julia (Porter) Dunham were:

1. ALONZO, who died at Johnsonburg, N. Y., October 9, 1869, leaving a widow, Harriett (Babbitt) and two children viz.: Mrs. Mary Shattuck and Herbert A., all of whom live at Warsaw, N. Y.

2. GEORGE H., who died at Johnsonburg, N. Y., May 31, 1894. He leaves a widow (second wife) and two children, by his first wife, Louisa (Virgin), viz.:

I. FRANK S., who is County Treasurer of Eddy County, North Dakota, and resides at New Rockford. He has two children, George H. and Fred. H.

II. FRED HALL, who is a lawyer at Batavia, N. Y., has three children, Leland Virgin, Mary B. and an infant.

III. FRANK, who died, when a young man, at Orangeville, N. Y.

Reuben left Hancock with his father's family in 1790 or '91, and went to Greenville, N. Y. He with his brother Joel, came to Livonia, N. Y., in the winter of 1809-10. He moved from there to Orangeville, Wyoming County, N. Y., in September, 1813, and settled on

MEMORANDA.

lot number 28, a parcel of the farm of nearly four-hundred acres, on which he lived more than fifty-five years. He was one of the early settlers; he was a leader and worker in the organization of the town, the placing of public roads, locating schools and organization of the first Presbyterian church in the town, of which he afterward became a useful member. He was one of the earliest dairymen on the Holland purchase, selling home manufactured cheese as early as 1823. He was a fair type of the Old Puritan stock from which he came. He held numerous town offices, the duties of which he always discharged with ability. His manner was pleasant and gentlemanly.

The writer remembers distinctly hearing him tell about going from Greenville, Green County, down to the landing, at Coxsacie, to see Robert Fulton come up the Hudson with the first steamboat. Reuben was at that time about seventeen years of age.

He spent his declining years with mental faculties unclouded, among firm friends and at home on the old farm.

The *Western New Yorker* published the following brief notice of his death:

STONE—In Orangeville, April 11th, 1869, Reuben Stone, aged 79 years.

The subject of this sketch was born in Hancock, Berkshire County, Mass., and moved to Orangeville in 1814, and has since resided on the same farm. He was a supporter of the Presbyterian Church from its organization, becoming a member about 1840. He was one of those honest, industrious, upright men whose whole life is a worthy example, and his last days were those of one whose hopes were well founded, and his death that of a Christian in full hope of immortality.

MEMORANDA.

(38)

IV. LEVINNIA was born at Greenville, N. Y., July 20, 1793, died at Greenville, N. Y., January 1, 1801.

(39)

V. LYMAN was born at Greenville, N. Y., October 22, 1797, and died at Ionia, Mich., April 27, 1880. He married April 5, 1821, at Orangeville, N. Y., Maria Vancize, a daughter of Simon Vancize, born May 17, 1804. She died at Muir, Mich., May 22, 1886.

Lyman moved from Greenville, N. Y., to Livonia, with his mother in 1812. As a man he was eccentric, original and interesting in conversation. A Michigan newspaper speaks of him as a man who could raise the largest potatoes, and spell the longest words of any man in Michigan.

(40)

VI. LEVINNIA was born at Greenville, N. Y., September 14, 1801, died June 12, 1803.

MEMORANDA.

Chapter IX.

(41)

I. HARRIET WARD was born at Guilford, Conn., December 21, 1786, and died at Honesdale, Pa., at the home of Mrs. Charlotte (Stone) Hand November 12, 1879. She never married. Was buried at Mt. Pleasant, Pa.

(42)

II. MARIA was born December 8, 1788, at Guilford, Conn., and died at Mt. Pleasant, Pa., April 27, 1852. She was single.

(43)

III. HENRY WARD was born at Guilford, Conn., May 17, 1791, and died at Honesdale, Pa., August 20, 1881. He married, July 24, 1823, Catharene Walch Niven of Newburg, N. Y., she was born at Newburg, August 28, 1801, and died at Mt. Pleasant, Pa., July 30, 1876. Her father was Major Daniel Niven, of General Washington's staff in the Revolutionary War. He was a civil engineer and planned an extension to the fortifications at West Point, his acquaintance with Lafayette was intimate, and lasted until his death.

He moved from Guilford, Conn., to Mt. Pleasant, Pa., when quite young. In 1818 he became a general merchant at that place, which business he continued in until 1846, when he removed to Honesdale, where

MEMORANDA.

he continued the same business. He retired from active life in 1867.

His acquaintance became very extended. He was known as a man of ability and sterling worth. He united with the Presbyterian church, and always was active in church work, and became a ruling elder. He retained his strength of mind body until his last illness, which was brief. He left a wide circle of friends and acquaintances to mourn the loss of an exceptional character. One of nature's noblemen.

> "His life was gentle, and the elements
> So mixed in him, that nature might stand up,
> And say to all the world—this was a man!"

(44)

IV. RACHEL was born March 26, 1796, and died January 28, 1797.

(45)

V. WILLIAM RUSSELL was born at Guilford, Conn., September 18, 1806, he died at Scranton, Pa., December 5, 1889, he married, November 21, 1832, Amanda Fowler, of Guilford, who was born at Guilford, Conn., September 19, 1805, and died at Scranton, Pa., April 27, 1881. They moved from Guilford to Mt. Pleasant, Pa., and located on a farm which business he continued to follow until 1870, when he retired from active business and lived at Scranton, Pa. He was an elder in the Presbyterian church at Mt. Pleasant and at Scranton.

MEMORANDA.

Chapter X.

Children of Timothy (32) and Anna (Griswold) Stone, all born
at Guilford, Conn.

(46)

1. REUBEN was born January 17, 1790, and died
April 8, 1863. He married, February 16, 1814, Lucinda
Camp, who was born January 27, 1793, and died
October 16, 1865.

Reuben was born in the old Caleb stone house at
the corner of Broad and River streets, and always
lived on this and the adjoining place. Reuben held
the office of town clerk in 1835, and was a magistrate
for a number of years, being appointed first in 1841,
three years after his father's term for the same office
expired. In 1845, '47, '48, and '49 he was chosen to
represent the Guilford District at the annual session
of the General Assembly of the State.

(47)

II. GEORGE was born June 22, 1791, and died
April 7, 1793.

(48)

III. TIMOTHY was born June 1, 1793, and died
very suddenly while at dinner at a hotel at Charles-
town, S. C., December 2, 1826. He married, September 19, 1824, Hannah Hubbard. She was born February 16, 1798, and died December 24, 1851. They had
no children.

MEMORANDA

(49)

IV. ANNA was born October 21, 1795, and died June 2, 1878. She never married.

(50)

V. GEORGE was born August 26, 1797, and died November 15, 1823. He was not married.

(51)

VI. LEVERETT was born February 24, 1799, and died October 25, 1816.

(52)

VII. ERASTUS was born December 3, 1800, and died October 1, 1802.

(53)

VIII. RICHARD was born June 6, 1802, and died May 8, 1869, at Great Bend, Pa. He married Henrietta Stevens of Springville, Pa. They had two children: 1st. George, who died at Dixon, Ill., leaving no family, and 2d. Anna Mary, who died at Great Bend, Pa., August 6, 1869, leaving no family.

(54)

IX. MARY BURGIS was born May 22, 1804, and died July 11, 1881. She never married.

(55)

X. ERASTUS was born April 8, 1812, and died April 11, 1812.

MEMORANDA.

Chapter XI.

(56)

I. AUSTIN was born June 2, 1801, at Homer, N. Y. He died October 9, 1881, at Westfield, Wis. He was married twice—first May 9, 1826, at Westfield, N. Y., to Harriet Tinker, who was born at Westfield, Mass., October 18, 1800, and died at Westfield, N. Y., April 27, 1829. She was a daughter of Joshua Tinker, born at Waterford, Conn., 1761, and Sally (Cowdry) Tinker, born April 8, 1784, at East Hadam, Conn. Joshua moved to Westfield, Mass., 1803; was a farmer and shoemaker. Austin married second at Westfield, N. Y., May 25, 1830, Maria Moore, who was born January 17, 1810, at Westfield, Mass., and died February 2, 1894, at Lansing, Mich. She was a niece of Harriet Tinker. Austin removed from Westfield, N Y., in 1837, to Pleasant Prairie, Wis., in 1839, to Racine, in 1842, to Kenosha, and 1856, to Westfield, Wis., where he lived the remainder of his life. He was the first superintendent of the Presbyterian Sunday-school at Westfield, N. Y. He was also Colonel of the militia at that place. After removing to Wisconsin he was a farmer, school-teacher, and carpenter. He held the office of town clerk, and other public positions. United with the Presbyterian church when quite young, and live a consistent, active Christian life. He was a great student, taking up the study of botany after he was sixty years of age. He analyzed all the flowers in the region of his home.

MEMORANDA.

(57)

II. RUSSELL was born at Homer, N. Y., July 26, 1803, and died at Fairwater, Wis., May 14, 1887. He married, October 12, 1826, Julia Ann Tower of Portland, N. Y. She was born May 1,1807, near Utica, N. Y., and died December 4, 1894, at Fairwater, Wis.

(58)

III. RHODA was born June 25, 1805, at Homer, N. Y. She died February 17, 1880, at Rochester, N. Y. She married, August 12, 1824, at Westfield, N. Y., Hiram Couch, who was born October 17, 1795, at Sandersfield, Berkshire County, Mass., and died at Westfield, N. Y., May 1, 1873. He came to Westfield, N. Y., from Massachusetts in 1815, with his father, William Couch and family. His ancestors were from Cornwall, Eng. Hiram was by trade a clothier, cloth dresser, and wool carder. This business he continued until his death. He, and Lester Stone (59) built a woolen factory one mile south of Westfield in 1848, which was operated by them until the death of Mr. Couch, when it passed into the hands of Lester Stone (59). Mr. Couch held numerous militia commissioned offices, all of which commissions are now in the hands of his son, Rev. Walter Varick Couch, of San Diego, Cal. Mr. Couch was an early member of the Presbyterian church in Westfield, and for many years one of its deacons. He was a strong temperance advocate. William Couch, Hiram's father, was a soldier in the Revolution. He was at Stillwater, Fort Plain, and New Haven. Was out in all about seven months.

(59)

IV. LESTER was born October 14, 1807, at Homer, N. Y. He married, June 4, 1833, Julia Brad-

MEMORANDA.

ley of Westfield, N. Y. She was born at Lebanon, N. Y., September 14, 1812, and died at Westfield, N. Y., June 5, 1889. Her grandfather was Abram Webster, who was a brother of Noah Webster of dictionary fame. Abram mortgaged his farm to assist his brother, Noah, in procuring an education.

Lester moved with his father's family from Homer, N. Y., to Westfield in February, 1813. They moved, by the way of Buffalo, just after the destruction of that city by the British. There was only one house left in all that city at that time. In 1848 he with his brother-in-law, Hiram Couch, built a woolen factory at Westfield, which he continued to operate until a few years ago. Lester is the last one of the seventh generation that is alive. He has been an active business man all his long life and the writer has received a number of communications from him in the last year (1895) that were written in a firm business hand. He is a member of the Presbyterian church at Westfield, N. Y., where he resides, his oldest daughter, Elizabeth Webster, keeping house for him.

(60)

V. ASA ATWATER was born at Homer, N. Y., December 3, 1810, and died at Cincinnati, Ohio, August 23, 1835. He was not married. He studied for the ministry, taught family school in Mississippi in slavery times, and was a strong abolitionist. He contributed several articles to New York papers that caused his removal from the South.

(61)

V. AMOS M. was born February 25, 1813, at Westfield, N. Y., and died November 14, 1862, at Clarkesville, Texas. He was twice married; first,

MEMORANDA.

January 3, 1838, at Nashville Tenn., to Jane McConnel, born November 26, 1817, in Ireland. She died October 7, 1846, at McMinnville, Tenn. He married the second time, November 3, 1847, Margaret L. Rodgers, who died at Clarksville, Texas, September 14, 1864. Amos was a minister of the Cumberland Presbyterian Church, was also president of Cumberland Female College at McMinnville, Tenn., from 1851 to 1855. In 1855 he removed with his family to Clarksville, Texas. He was pastor of the Cumberland Presbyterian Church there for several years. In the fall of 1859 he removed temporarily to San Antonio, Texas, where he remained one year, then returned to his home at Clarksville. During the War he was a Unionist.

(62)

VII. MARTHA was born at Westfield, N. Y., January 18, 1823, and died August 17, 1823.

(63)

VIII. MARY was born January 15, 1823, and died August 20, 1823.

(64)

IX. JOSHUA was born October 21, 1824, at Westfield, N. Y., and died at Greenfield, Mass., September 1, 1859. He married, November 8, 1855, Eliza L. Ingersoll of Greenfield, Mass., who was a daughter of Charles Ingersoll. Joshua was a homœopathic physician. They had no children.

MEMORANDA.

EIGHTH GENERATION.

Chapter XII.

Children of Joel (35) and Lucinda (Warner) Stone, all born at
Livonia, N. Y.

(65)

I. MORRIS WARNER was born April 22, 1810,
and died April 25, 1838, at Livonia, N. Y. He married in November, 1836, Margaret Reed. who died
June 6, 1851. They had one child, Morris, born
December 31, 1837, and died in January or February,
1839.

(66)

II. JOHN RUSSELL was born June 6, 1815, and
died August 20, 1842. He never married. He was a
miller by trade. He and his uncle, Orlando Warner,
built a grist mill, which he continued to own and
operate until his death.

(67)

III. JOEL was born October 30, 1820, and died
April 20, 1885. He married, March 14, 1850, Anna
Stone (86) a daughter of Lyman Stone (39). She was
born January 19, 1827, at Orangeville, N. Y., and now
resides with her son, Russell, at Livonia. N. Y.

Joel was a very successful farmer and a good finan-
cier. He was one of the original founders of the salt
industry at Lakeville, Livingston County. N. Y.;
being the president of the Company. He was Super-

MEMORANDA

visor of his town for several years. About a year before he died he purchased a house at Livonia, remodeled and furnished it throughout and made the Presbyterian Society at that place a present of it. It is used by the church for holding socials and any kind of gatherings that the society may think proper; the building is now called Stone Hall.

(68)

IV. REUBEN was born October 27, 1823, and died January 5, 1875, at Livonia, N. Y. He never married. He lived with his brother, Joel, with whom he was in partnership until his death. They carried on an extensive farming business. He like his brother was a very industrious man, and accumulated a fortune.

MEMORANDA.

Chapter XIII.

(69)

I. DARIUS was born September 3), 1812, at
Greenville, N. Y., and died at Ionia, Mich., March 14,
1888. He was married twice, first February 23, 1832,
at Geneseo, N. Y., to Mahala Norton, who was born
November 13, 1811, and died at Ionia, Mich., May 14,
1865. He married for a second wife, July 11, 1866,
Caroline C. Cleveland, who was born May 19, 1821.
She now resides at Ionia, Michigan.

When Darius was a few months old the family
moved from Greenville to the, then, new country at
Livonia, where he was reared. After his first marriage he lived on a farm of his father's at Orangeville, and the homestead at Livonia. After the father's death, Darius being eldest was chosen by his
brother and sisters to divide the estate which they
settled among themselves. He was likewise chosen
again in his sister Clarissa's estate in 1864. In the
spring of 1846, he and his brother came to Ionia,
Michigan, where he purchased some land. He went
back and in the fall moved his family to the new
home. The journey was made overland, coming
across Lake Erie and from Detroit it was through an
almost unbroken wilderness. They arrived at Ionia
in October, 1846. At that time the place was all forest, but years of hard toil made a beautiful farm of
several hundred acres. He was one of the charter mem-

MEMORANDA.

DARIUS STONE.

bers in the organization, in 1857, of the Church of the Disciples, at Muir, Michigan, and was a consistent Christian man.

(70)

II. CLARRISSA was born July 15, 1814, at Livonia, N. Y., and died February 7, 1864, at North Plains, Mich. She married, March 12, 1835, Tobias H. Perrine, who was born in Seneca County, N. Y., and died at North Plains, Mich. They had no children.

Children of Orin (36) and Betsey (Cowel) Stone all born at Livonia, N. Y.

(71)

I. BETSEY ANN was born June 12, 1817, and died January 8, 1884, at Pardee, Kan. She married, November 3, 1841, Daniel Calkins, who was born in Livonia. N. Y., April 5, 1818, and died at Hoytville, Mich., May 14, 1892. They were farmers.

(72)

II. POLLY SAMANTHA was born October 3, 1820, and died March 5, 1892, at Ionia, Mich. She married, December 7, 1840, Levi F. Burdick, who was born March 22, 1814, at Avon, Livingston County, N. Y., and died January 15, 1888, at Ionia, Mich. Mr. Burdick was a farmer. They were members of the Church of Christ, of which he was a deacon.

(73)

III. JOHN RUSSELL was born April 30, 1823. He married, May 15, 1845, at Livonia, N. Y., Mary

MEMORANDA.

Ann McClintick*, born December 1, 1822, at Livonia, N. Y. They reside at Barnes, Kan. He has held the office of justice of the peace; is a farmer and member of the Church of Christ.

(74)

IV. SARAH A. was born May 10, 1828. She was married, November 22, 1849, at Ionia, Mich., to John Chase, who was born at Coxsackie, N. Y., March 5, 1822, and died at Ionia, Mich., March 9, 1890. He was a farmer and a member of the Church of Christ. She now resides at Ionia, Mich., with her son, James Chase.

---

* She died at Barnes, Kan., April 11, 1896.

MEMORANDA.

Chapter XIV.

(75)

I. LOIS was born July 18. 1816. She married, June 2, 1841, Obadiah Tilton. who was born in Orangeville, N. Y., January 27, 1817, and died October 24. 1886. He was a son of John Tilton. With the exception of about five years. Mr. Tilton spent his entire life in Orangeville. following farming and dairying, and also owned and operated a cheese factory for a few years. He located soon after marriage on lot No. 52. He held the office of assessor for nine years in succession and was supervisor of his town in 1870-71. Lois now resides on the farm with her eldest son, James.

The following notice of the death of Mr. Tilton was published in the *Western New Yorker:*

TILTON—The sudden death of Obadiah Tilton occurred October 24. and was simply announced in our last issue. Mr. Tilton was born in Orangeville, January 27, 1817. June 2. 1841. he married Lois Stone, eldest daughter of Reuben Stone. late of Orangeville. Soon after their marriage they removed to Indiana. where they resided five years. Except for this interval Mr. Tilton's entire life was spent in Orangeville. and since his settlement here. on one section of land. A well cultivated farm and commodious and valuable farm buildings attest his thorough efficiency as a business man. Without inherited wealth, his persevering industry, unquestioned integ-

MEMORANDA.

HARVEY STONE.

rity and genuine good sense, early gained him a competency. Mr. Tilton held many places of trust and responsibility. As a public officer he served with credit and ability, securing the entire approval of those he represented. Ever at the front in temperance work, faithfully trying to raise the unfortunate and fallen, he was ever ready to aid with money, time and influence, this great work. Though nearly seventy years old, his untiring energy made him appear much younger. His life was characterized by industry and integrity. He was a regular attendant of religious services and contributed liberally to all benevolent purposes. An esteemed citizen, a loyal friend, a kind husband and father, and a worthy man has been taken from among us.

(76)

II. HARVEY was born February 14, 1818, and died January 7, 1887, in Orangeville, N. Y., where he had always lived. He married, February 20, 1840, Eliza Lewis, who was born in Orangeville, N. Y., February 20, 1820. She was a daughter of the Hon. Truman Lewis, who was born at New Hartford, Conn., November 5, 1784. He left his father's house at Vernon, N. Y., in the spring of 1807, and made his way on foot, much of the way being through a wilderness, to Orangeville, Wyoming County, N. Y., where he bought some land in what was then an almost unbroken forest. This farm he owned when he died. Here he and his wife literally hewed out for themselves and their children a home. He was a member of the Presbyterian Church. In the War of 1812 he was in active service, holding the commission of ensign from Governor Daniel D. Tompkins. He was frequently elected to important town offices. He represented Genesee County in the Legislature in 1834-35, and was the first treasurer of Wyoming County.

MEMORANDA

For something like fifteen years he was the agent for Wyoming County of the Farmers' Loan and Trust Company of New York, and for the town of Orangeville of the Trustees under the will of James Loyd deceased, of Boston, Mass. These parties were the successors of the Old Holland Land Company, and at the time they held a very large number of mortgages and owned a great number of farms' in that part of Wyoming County, included in the Holland Land Company's purchase. This business entrusted to him was therefore one of great magnitude. He so discharged his duties, however, as to both merit, and receive the most gratifying commendation of the companies he represented, and the thanks and confidence of all persons occupying these lands, and liable to pay these mortgages, who everywhere expressed their gratitude for his kindness and forebearance, their perfect faith in his integrity and justice.

After closing up his business he moved to Warsaw, N. Y., and spent the last seven years of his life with his son, Simeon D. Lewis, at whose home he died, September 15, 1865. He was a man of great executive ability, of eminent good judgment, and of the strictest integrity. He was also a genial, companionable man, possessing an inexhaustible fund of anecdotes, with which he often entertained his friends. He married, October 3, 1811, Lucy Porter, who was born March 6, 1795. She was the daughter of Seth Porter and Sarah (Cowles) Porter and a granddaughter of Captain John Porter. She (Lucy) died at Rockford, Ill., December 13, 1866. Truman was a descendant of William Lewis, who came from Braintree, England, in the ship, Lion, landing at Boston, Mass., September 16, 1632.

Eliza died October 15, 1894, and her brother,

MEMORANDA.

Simeon D. Lewis of Warsaw., Y., wrote the following obituary:

Mrs. Eliza Lewis Stone was the daughter of Hon. Truman Lewis, one of the pioneers of Wyoming county. She was born February 20th, 1820, in the town of Orangeville, where she always lived.

At the time of her birth the struggles of her parents for a comfortable home were by no means ended. When we remember also that she was five years old when De Witt Clinton made his memorable journey from Albany to Buffalo on the Erie canal; that she was ten years old when the first short railroad was built in this country, and that she was twenty-five years old when Morse first exhibited to the world the wonders of the telegraph; we can easily understand that in her younger days her environment was unfavorable to a liberal education, and that in this respect she was limited to the curriculum of the district school. She was, however, a great reader, and was therefore, to the last a woman of unusual intelligence —keeping constantly abreast of the times in current literature, and the general news of the day.

On her 20th birthday she was united in marriage to Harvey Stone, and bravely began with him a struggle for a home and a competence, in which effort they were reasonably successful.

She had three children—Mrs. George L. Parker, of Buffalo; Morris L. Stone, of Wamego, Kansas, and Truman L. Stone, of Orangeville, with whom she has lived since the death of her husband in 1887.

She was a woman of cheerful temper, kind to all, sympathetic with all who were in trouble, and ever ready to aid the unfortunate, and do what she could to relieve those who were in distress.

The legitimate fruits of a long life so filled with good deeds, was a large circle of devoted friends, who mourn her departure. In her christian character, she was a woman of deeds rather than of professions. She was not one of those who on the street corners cried, "Lord, Lord," but rather one who did the will of her Heavenly Father.

MEMORANDA.

For several years she has been an invalid; at times a sufferer, and recently almost helpless, but through all these weary months and years she has been cheerful, and has ever seemed disposed to look on the bright side of life.

In the remembrance of her broad charity, her cheerful disposition, her life filled with good deeds, and her love for all that is good and bright and beautiful her children have a priceless legacy.

The spring after his (Harvey's) marriage he bought some land of his father, Reuben (37). He lived on this farm until the winter of 1844, when he sold this farm and purchased of his father-in-law (Truman Lewis), who was agent for the Trustees under the will of James Loyd, deceased, of Boston, Mass., a farm on lot No. 58, in Orangeville, N. Y. He afterward bought more land so that he had a large farm. He built good buildings and lived on this farm in comparative comfort all his life. He held the office of supervisor in 1855, was a justice of the peace for twelve years, and justice of sessions for the county two terms. He loved his country and its civil institutions. While a boy at school he wrote an essay which was long, and prophesied with uncommon clearness that the final result of slavery in this country would be war and bloodshed, which prophecy proved only too true. He was a man of sterling virtues. Among these may be mentioned remarkable uprightness of character, and he possessed a great dislike for anything petty or mean.

He was ever ready to oblige when it could be done without sacrifice of principle, but could not give up his own personal opinions. He attended and supported the Presbyterian church. He and his wife lie peacefully side by side in the cemetery at Johnsonburg,

MEMORANDA.

N. Y., in which place they attended church for more than thirty years.

The *Western New Yorker* published the following notices of their deaths:

January 11, 1887.

HARVEY STONE died at his home in the town of Orangeville, January 7th, the funeral obsequies taking place at Johnsonburg on the 9th, attended by a very large collection of commemorating neighbors and friends from adjoining towns. Reuben Stone, father of the deceased, was an early pioneer of the town, locating in 1811, from Livonia, Livingston County, N. Y. Mr. Stone was truly a native of the town in which he had lived from birth, born on the premises where his father first located, February 14th, 1818. A representative citizen, meriting and retaining the confidence of a community most familiar with him, was the recipient of all the town offices at various periods, except town clerk and collector. For two terms presided on the bench as justice of sessions. His industry and exertions largely promoted the clearing up and prosperity of the town. Among the first to introduce extended dairy manufacture of cheese, that placed a backward locality in the list of competing agricultural advance. The demised had been a victim of paralysis for three years previous to his death, during the time gradually failing, subjected to lingering disease and helpless prostration, finally prostrated a strong frame and healthy constitution that had endured the hardships incident to the occupation of farmer, whose examples were not without merit. His genial deportment will not fail to be remembered by all with whom he associated. Meeting acquaintances always cordial, in contact with strangers equally genial. Always a well provided home furnished an open door of welcome and hospitality. A widow wife survives to mourn his absence, one daughter, Mrs. George L. Parker, of Buffalo, and two

MEMORANDA.

sons, M. L. Stone, of Wamego, Kansas, and T. L. Stone, present keeper of the Wyoming County Poorhouse.

Thursday, October 18, 1894.

MRS. ELIZA STONE.—Died at Varysburg on the 15th inst., age 74 years. Mrs. Stone was the widow of Harvey Stone, deceased. mother of Truman Lewis Stone, and sister of S. D. Lewis, of this place. For several years she has been an invalid and for a long time almost helpless, but has had the tenderest care from her son and his wife. with whom she has lived since the death of her husband. Mrs. Stone leaves two other children, Mrs. George L. Parker, of Buffalo, and M. L. Stone, of Wamego, Kansas. In her case also it is demonstrated that a long and useful life brings its legitimate fruitage in a large circle of friends, who will long remember her gentle nature and her many acts of kindness. The funeral will be attended on Thursday, the 18th. at 2 o'clock p. m. from her son's residence.

The personal characteristics of Mr. Stone best appear in the following letters to the writer from the Hon. A. J. Lorish, County Judge of Wyoming County, and S. D. Lewis, a life-long resident of the county:

Warsaw, N. Y., August 12, 1896.

Mr. T. L. Stone:

Dear Friend:—I hear you are contemplating writing up and publishing a life of your father, and I want to contribute a few words. I went into Judge Corlett's office in Attica, as a law-student in 1857; and, as was the case with all law-students in those days, I was expected to pettifog all justice's court matters coming into the office; and with a copy of Blackstone under my arm, I traveled all over that region and became acquainted with every justice of the peace for miles around. One day I was directed by the judge to go up

MEMORANDA.

before Esq. Stone of Orangeville, and try a law-suit. He explained to me the matter and advised me what to do. I asked him who would be against me, and was told Blackmer, Henshaw or Gladding and, perhaps, all combined. I was startled, for all those gentlemen were giants in justices' court, in those days. Judge Corlett noticed my terror, — said encouragingly, "Don't be scared! Harve Stone," as he was familiarly called, "presides in and runs his own court, and no party in a suit before him, fails to receive justice no matter who his lawyer is, or who is against him, and he won't see you harmed." Thus assured, I went and tried the case, and found Esq. Stone just as Corlett had said, and in the many times after that I appeared in his court, I had additional evidence that impartial justice was always dealt out to suitors. He was remarkable along that line. He could grasp the question in dispute and readily see what justice required, and was fearless in administering it. He never permitted technicalities to stand in the way; but, before resorting to trial, he sat, in all matters of dispute between his neighbors, as a mediator and a peacemaker. The same independence and fearlessness that characterized his official acts was seen in his politcal life. He was always ready, when disagreeing with old political associates, to give a reason for the faith that was in him. His large commanding presence and personal address, with an inexhaustible fund of good humor and agreeable conversational powers, made him a welcome party in any gathering. Everybody conceded conscientiousness and honesty to the acts of Harvey Stone, whether personal, judicial or political.   Yours, etc.,

ANDREW J. LORISH.

MEMORANDA

Warsaw, N. Y., August 7, 1896.

Truman L. Stone, Esq., Varysburg, N. Y.:

Dear Nephew—Kindly accept the following as a
brief response to your letter of recent date, asking me
to give you some characteristics of your father and
grandfather.

My recollections of Reuben Stone are very clear
and distinct. He was a typical pioneer of New England birth, who brought into the wilderness of Western New York, a sturdy independence of character;
that patient industry, which changed the unbroken
forest into fruitful fields; and that love for every good
institution, which made him a faithful, active supporter of schools, the Christian church, and every
other organized effort to educate and elevate the race.
He was a man of independent thought—one who
formed his own opinions, and believed most implicitly
in the correctness of his own conclusions. By his
industry, frugality and good management, he achieved
success in his chosen occupation. As a neighbor, he
was kind and generous, and in his family, loved and
venerated. His second wife was sister to my mother,
and as his farm joined that of my father, the relations
of the two families were quite close and intimate. In
olden times he was a whig in politics, and for years
Truman Lewis and Reuben Stone were elected over-
seers of the poor for the town of Orangeville on the
same ticket. In many ways your father, Harvey
Stone, resembled his father, Reuben. He was perhaps somewhat more social, a man of wider acquaintance, and more inclined to keep step with modern
methods, and one whose mental vision took in a
wider sweep. Like him he was a man of positive
convictions touching all questions, and he always

MEMORANDA.

stood ready to maintain them fearlessly. He married my sister, Eliza, on her twentieth birthday, and together with brave hearts, and strong and tireless hands, they commenced to carve out their fortunes. In this respect, like your grandfather, they were reasonably successful. They acquired a modest indepedence, not by a skillful shuffling of financial cards, but by an intelligent use of the means at hand, and by a determined tireless industry.

Harvey Stone held several important town offices. If I remember correctly he was at different times high way commissioner, justice of the peace, and supervisor; and at least for one term, he was called by the electors of Wyoming County to the office of sessions justice. You certainly can look back upon your ancestry with pride.

While such men's names are not always written in flaming characters on historic pages, it is nevertheless true that in more respects than one, their lives are heroic. When we recall their limitations, and remember their interest in others, and their labors freely given for others, as well as their successful struggles against every obstacle standing between them and their hope, we may well apply to their lives, these words of Wordsworth:

> "Life I repeat is energy of love,
>   Divine or human; exercised in pain,
>   In strife, and tribulation; and ordained
>   If so approved and sanctified, to pass
>   Through shades and silent rest, to endless joy."

Yours truly,

S. D. LEWIS.

MEMORANDA.

(77)

III. SARAH was born October 28, 1820, and died at Portland, Mich., January 15, 1871. She married, April 21, 1854, Lester W. Sparks of North Plains, Mich., who was born June 11, 1811, at Syracuse, N. Y., and died July 30, 1882, at Grenola, Kan. He was a farmer. He lived in North Plains, Portland, Mich., and Grenola, Kansas.

(78)

IV. LUCINDA was born in 1822, and died October 6, 1825.

(79)

V. REUBEN was born 1824, and died October 11, 1825.

(80)

VI. LUCINDA was born September 28, 1826, and died March 15, 1858. She married, May ——, 1850, Hiram Smith, who was born in Orangeville, N. Y., February 19, 1829, and died at Wabaunsee, Kansas, May 25, 1879. He was a farmer.

(81)

VII. CAROLINE was born December 22, 1828, and died January 20, 1881, at Wabaunsee, Kansas. She never married.

MEMORANDA.

Children of Reuben (37) and Julia (Dunham) Stone, all born at Orangeville, N. Y.

(82)

I. EDWIN was born April 17, 1833. He married, January 1, 1856, Emma Crawford, who was born at Phelps, Ontario County, N. Y., September 11, 1837. They are farmers and reside in Orangeville, N. Y. After his father (Reuben) died, he purchased the old homestead, where he now resides.

(83)

II. LUCY CLARRISSA was born January 22, 1838. She married, March 26, 1856, George Hoy, who was born March 1, 1832, in the County of Monnon, Ireland. He died October 21, 1892, at Johnsonsburg, N. Y. Mr. Hoy when seventeen years of age emigrated to America, landing in New York in the spring of 1849. He came direct to Rochester, N. Y. He worked for a wealthy farmer in Ontario County for three years. He then procured a position as foreman on a large farm at Pittsford, Monroe County, which he held for three years. He came to Orangeville, Wyoming County, N. Y., early in the spring of 1855, and bought sixty acres of land on lot No. 44. Soon after he purchased land adjoining, so that he had a farm of over two hundred acres. Soon after marriage he commenced making dairy cheese for Rochester market. In 1858 he commenced buying cheese on speculation, which business he followed the rest of his life. In the spring of 1864 he erected a cheese factory at Johnsonsburg, N. Y., being the first one built west of Herkimer County. He afterward bought other factories and formed what is yet known as the Johnsonburg combination of factories. He was well known

MEMORANDA.

throughout the United States and Liverpool, Eng., in cheese circles, and was often alluded to as the *Cheese King*. He was elected three times to the office of supervisor of his town, and when he died he had nearly one thousand acres of farms, real estate in the city of Buffalo and other cities and a large amount of personal property. He was a director of the Citizen's Bank of Arcade. His life financially was a grand success. He attended and supported the Presbyterian church, and was a most liberal contributor to every kind of charity. Lucy now resides at her home in Johnsonsburg, N. Y., and is one of the leading members of the Presbyterian church at that place.

MEMORANDA.

GEORGE HOY.

Chapter XV.

Children of Lyman (33) and Maria (Vancize) Stone, all born at Orangeville, N. Y.

(84)

I. ALFRED was born January 2, 1822. He has been married three times: first January 6, 1847, at Java, Wyoming County, N. Y., to Betsey Maria Carpenter, who was born in 1828, and died at Essex, Clinton County, Mich., November 19, 1859. He married second time at Essex, Mich., January 1, 1860, Lydia Ann Lane, who was born November 6, 1827, in Alllegany County, N. Y., and died at Parrinton, Mich., December 12, 1882. He married third time, May 17, 1885, Rebecca Beck, who was born in England, February 27, 1826. Mr. Stone is by occupation a farmer. His farm is in the corporation of Parrinton, Mich. He has been very fond of hunting and trapping, having caught five lynx in one season, also killed a great many deer and bear. He resides at Parrinton, Mich.

(85)

II. LAVINIA was born February 2, 1825. She married, February 14, 1854, at Ionia., Mich., Martin Hubbell, who was born October 4, 1824; they are both members of the Presbyterian church. They are farmers and reside at Muir, Mich.

(86)

III. ANNA was born January 19, 1827. She married, March 14, 1850, Joel Stone (67) who was born

MEMORANDA

October 30, 1820, and died April 20, 1885. Anna resides with her eldest son, Russell, at Livonia, N. Y. She is a member of the Presbyterian church.

(87)

IV. BANI was born August 15, 1828, and died at Canon, Mich., June 23, 1848. He was not married.

(88)

V. RHODA was born December 23, 1833, and died at Ionia, Mich., December 29, 1855. She married in 1854, Newton Tibbetts of Ionia, Mich. He survived his wife a few years. They had no children.

MEMORANDA.

Chapter XVI

Children of Henry Ward (43) and Catherine Walch (Niven) Stone, all
born at Mt. Pleasant, Pa.

(89)

I. CHARLES NIVEN was born August 21, 1824,
and died January 1, 1830.

(90)

II. HARRIET WARD was born June 15, 1826,
and died at Honesdale, Pa.. May 24, 1884. She married, April 3, 1845, Hon. Charles Philips Waller, who
was born at Wilkes Barre, Pa., August 7, 1819, and
died at Honesdale, Pa., August 18, 1882. He was a
lawyer and at his death presiding judge of the 22d
Judicial District comprising the counties of Wayne
and Pike, Pa. He was educated at Williams College,
and was a prominent resident of Wayne County from
the time he commenced practicing law.

(91)

III. JANE ELIZABETH was born January 21,
1829, and died March 9, 1868. at Honesdale, Pa. She
married, January 10, 1854, at Honesdale, Pa., Marcus
Sayre of Newark, N. J. He is a member of the Marcus Sayre Company, dealers in masons' materials.
He resides at Montrose, N. J.

(143)

MEMORANDA.

(92)

IV. CHARLOTTE NIVEN was born July 17, 1831. She married, October 3, 1854, Horace Chapman Hand of Honesdale, Pa., who was born May 15, 1830, at Windham, N. Y. Mr. Hand is the cashier of the Wayne County Savings Bank at Honesdale, Pa. He is an elder in the Presbyterian church, and a man commanding the respect of the community in which he lives.

(93)

V. JANNETT SCOTT was born September 3, 1833, and died at Honesdale, Pa., July 14, 1885. She married, October 3, 1854, Edwin Fuller Torrey of Honesdale, Pa. He was born June 4, 1832. He for a time was the proprietor of the Honesdale Mills and engaged in the wholesale feed business. He is now the cashier of the Honesdale National Bank.

(94)

VI. WILLIAM HENRY was born October 1, 1835. He married, January 22, 1873, Cornelia S. Short, who was born March 28, 1843, at Cincinnatus, Cortland County, N. Y. He is general insurance agent and notary public. They reside at Honesdale, Pa. They have no children.

(95)

VII. MARY BLAKE was born July 26, 1838, and died April 17, 1853.

MEMORANDA.

Chapter XVII.

(96)

I. HENRY AUGUSTUS was born November 24, 1835, and died January 25, 1864. He was not married.

(97)

II. CHARLES RUSSELL was born December 6, 1837. He was drowned June 13, 1860. He was not married.

(98)

III. HENRIETTA FOWLER was born December 12, 1839. She never married. Now resides with her brother, George Elliot Stone, at Danville, Va.

(99)

IV. JOHN WARD was born April 10, 1842, and died August 4, 1861. He was single.

(100)

V. CATHERINE ELLIOT was born July 20, 1844, and died October 7, 1844.

(101)

VI. CATHERINE ELIZABETH was born September 28, 1845, and died June 22, 1863. She was single.

MEMORANDA.

(102)

VII. GEORGE ELLIOT was born January 21, 1850. He married, September 25, 1873, Martha Kays. She was born November 14, 1854. They reside at Danville, Va.* He is one of the firm of John G. Lea & Co., proprietors of the Banner Warehouse of that place, for the sale of leaf tobacco, at Danville, Va.

———

*They removed to Greensborough, N. C., in 1895, where they now reside.

MEMORANDA.

Chapter XVIII.

**Children of Reuben (46) and Lucinda (Camp) Stone, all born at
Guilford, Conn.**

(103)

I. ELIZABETH was born November 18, 1815, and
died March 11, 1817.

(104)

II. LEVERETT CAMP was born June 4, 1819,
and died June 12, 1892. He married, November 14,
1853, Adeline Eliot Griswold. She was born June 28,
1816. She is a descendant of the Rev. Joseph Elliot,
who was born at Roxbury, Mass., December 20, 1638.
He was graduated from Harvard in 1658. In 1664 he
was settled in Guilford, where he continued to reside
till his death, which occurred in May, 1694. He, at
the time he moved to Guilford, undoubtedly purchased a part or all of John Stone's (2) allotment, a part
of which was afterward sold off, and became the home
of the late Dr. Talcott. Mrs. Stone now resides in the
house which Timothy (32) speaks of in a letter written
to Eber (34) as the house built for Brother Bille. This
house stands on the lot first purchased by Caleb (13)
of John Leete in 1714. The house was erected in 1769,
but has been remodeled since that time. Mrs. Stone
is an invalid; her daughter Anna lives with her. Mrs.
Stone is of a cheerful disposition, and looks on the
bright side of life. Leverett was born on the old
home lot. Mr. Stone was educated in common

MEMORANDA

schools, but was remarkably well read. He was by occupation a farmer. In his youth he taught school winters. He was a Selectman at two different times, for several years. He held the office of Justice of the Peace several terms. Also that of Registrar. He was a man highly respected by his neighbors and friends.

(105)

III. LUCINDA CAMP was born November 17, 1825, and died December 13, 1825.

(106)

IV. HENRY BURRIT was born December 15, 1821, and died April 2, 1823.

(107)

V. REUBEN HENRY was born June 23, 1829. He married, March 5, 1874, at Kansas City, Mo., Carrie D. Robinson, who was born February 27, 1839, in Morgan County, Mo. They reside at Los Angeles, Cal. They have one child.

I. Lucy Camp, who was born July 28, 1875. She is single.

MEMORANDA.

Chapter XIX.

(108

I. ORLANDO S. was born April 29, 1827, and
died December 5, 1830.

(109)

II. WILLIAM TINKER was born September 11,
1828, in Westfield, N. Y.   He married, at Aurora, Ill.,
August 2, 1866. Eliza Jane Wright, who was born in
Ireland, July 25, 1840.   They now reside at 278 Jackson Street, Aurora, Ill.   Mr. Stone, when thirteen
years of age, was apprenticed to Mr. C. J. J. Ingersoll, publisher of the "Westfield Messenger," published at Westfield, N. Y.   It was in this printing
office that he set his first stick of type.   He worked
here five years when he went to Worcester, Mass.,
and worked on Burritt's "Christian Citizen," a paper
at that time of wide circulation.   In 1854 he went to
Boston, Mass., and worked in the office of T. R. Mar-
vin & Son, publishers of the "Missionary Herald."   In
1860 he worked in the book establishment of H. O.
Houghton & Co., Cambridge.   He then went West
working on a number of newspapers, finally going to
work on the "Aurora Herald and Daily Express,"
where he has been for more than twenty-five years.
He has written articles editorially on the current lit-

MEMORANDA.

crature of the day, also on Theology. He met with an accident when quite young, which destroyed the sense of hearing—

"And pleased and pleasing let me live
With merry heart that laughs at care."

(110)

Children of Austin (56) and Maria (Moore) Stone.

I. LEANDER was born at Westfield, N. Y., November 23, 1831, and died at Chicago, Ill., April 2, 1888. He married, March 7, 1855, at Kenosha, Wis., Harriet H. Leonard, who was born March 5, 1832, in Yruxton, Cortland County, N. Y. She now resides at 3352 Indiana Avenue, Chicago, Ill. Mr. Stone was a school teacher for six years, then editor and proprietor of the "Kenosha Telegraph." He subsequently moved to Chicago, where he was editor of a newspaper, a member of the board of education and church clerk until his death. His wife was the youngest child of Addison and Elizabeth (Clark) Leonard of Hartford, Conn. Both her grandfathers served in the Revolution and Addison Leonard in the War of 1812. Mrs. Stone is now and has been for twenty years president of the Young Women's Christian Association, of Chicago. She is now (1895) overseeing the erection of their large building on Michigan Avenue and Lake front.

(111)

II. HARRIET MARIA was born at Westfield, N. Y., January 16, 1834, and died at Kenosha, Wis.,

MEMORANDA.

May 23, 1867. She married at Kenosha, March 7
1855, Henry C. Dodge, who was born at Hartland,
Windsor County, Vt., April 28, 1833.   He is the secretary of the Whitaker Engine and Skein Company,
and resides at Kenosha, Wis.

(112)

III. LINNAENS XENOPHEN was born at Westfield, N. Y., August 16, 1836, and died at Kenosha,
Wis., January 26, 1845.

(113)

IV. HUMPHEY DAVY was born at Racine,
Wis., April 25, 1839, and died at Pleasant Prairie,
Wis., August 7, 1841.

(114)

V. HIRAM LESTER was born at Pleasnt Prairie,
Wis., March 1, 1841, and died at Atlanta. Ga., July
28, 1864. He married, September 10, 1863, at Westfield, Wis., Caroline Page. He enlisted in Co. E., 16th
Regiment Wisconsin Volunteers in the spring of 1861,
at Westfield, Wis.   After serving three years re-enlisted, becoming a veteran.   He was with Sherman on
his march to the sea; was wounded at Atlanta, Ga.,
July 21, 1864, and died a week later.   He was buried
in Georgia.   They had no children.

(115)

VI. MARY JANE was born at Kenosha, Wis.,
December 30, 1844, and died at Warrens Mills, Wis.,
March 23, 1872.   She married, March 29, 1868, at
Westfield, Wis., Lewis Brainard Bridgman, who was
born in Wisconsin, November 8, 1845.   He is a son of
Noah, who was a descendant of John Bridgman.   He
is a farmer, and resides at Wakonda, S. D.

MEMORANDA.

(116)

VII. PARMENAS AUGUSTINE was born at Kenosha, Wis., November 16, 1848. He married, October 13, 1875, at Rochester, N. Y., Harriet Abbie Gibbs, who was born June 6, 1850, a daughter of George W. Gibbs, born at Milford, Mass., October, 1806, and Catherine (Winch) born at Franklin, Mass., May 22, 1800. She was a music teacher before marriage. Parmenas, at the age of 17, began teaching district school. Afterward attended Ripon College for eighteen months, then studied music under George F. Root, P. P. Bliss, and others. For several years he taught singing classes, and conducted musical conventions. He subsequently engaged in the book business, and traveled several years for a publishing house. They are members of the Plymouth Congregational Church at Lansing, Mich. He is the superintendent of the Sunday School.

MEMORANDA.

Chapter XX.

(117)

I. FRANKLIN was born August 27, and died at Alto, Wis., January, 1886.   He never married.

(118)

II. ELI was born June 25, 1831, and died August 15, 1832.

(119)

III. RHODA E. was born March 3, 1833, and died at Alto, Wis., October 26, 1868.   She was single.

(120)

IV. HARRIETT was born June 4, 1836, and died June 26, 1836.

(121)

V. HENRY was born June 4, 1836, and died December 20, 1863.   He was single.

(122)

VI. EDWARD P. was born December 4 1837.   He was married twice, first March, 1862, to Annias Larrabee, who died June, 1887; second, January, 1891, to Sylphina Larrabee.

(123)

VII. FRANCIS was born October 28, 1839, and died March 13, 1855.

MEMORANDA

(124)

VIII. NELLIE was born October 21, 1841, at Westfield, N. Y. She has been married twice. First, February 22, 1863, to Edward A. Knight, at Alto, Wis., who was born March 27, 1828, and died February 22, 1865, at Center Creek, Minn. He was a farmer; and second, January 1, 1871, at Center Creek, Minn., to Rev. Orson O. Rundell, who was born January 12, 1847, in Lake County, Ill. She now resides at Princeton, Idaho. Mr. Rundell's grandparents came from France. Both of his grandfathers were ministers of the Gospel. He was a Congregational minister.

(125)

IX. HELEN M. was born April 5, 1846. She has been a teacher in high school at Escanaba, Mich., and at Sheboygan, Wis. She now resides temporarily at Britt, Iowa. She is single.

(126)

X. MELVA M. was born April 1, 1848, and died May, 1888, at Alto, Wis. She was single.

(127)

XI. GEORGE F. was born in Alto, Wis., April 14, 1850. He married Bell C. Blanchard, who was born July 30, 1863. They have no children. He is in the insurance business. They reside at Britt, Iowa.

MEMORANDA.

Chapter XXI.

**Children of Hiram and Rhoda (58) (Stone) Couch, all born at
Westfield, N. Y.**

(128)

I. HENRY LANSING was born September 17,
1825. He married, June 4, 1857, Susan Anthony
Dederer, who was born at Blauvelt, Rockland County,
N. Y. Her parents were from prominent families of
Rockland County. Her paternal grandfather was for
years engaged in the West India trade. Her maternal
grandfather was Judge Cornelius I. Blauvelt, one of
the oldest, best known, and wealthiest citizens of
Rockland County, N. Y.

Mr. Couch was educated in common schools and
Westfield Academy, New York. At the age of eighteen years he entered a clerkship in a store at Westfield,
N. Y., that was connected with a large manufactory of
farming tools, where he remained two years. He then
entered a store at Oriskany Falls, N. Y., and from there
he returned to Westfield, N. Y., and entered into a co-
partnership with George W. & John A. Couch, as general merchants. At the end of one year he sold out his
interest and in 1854 went to New York City, where h
was employed in the general freight department of
the New York & Erie Railroad Co. After a time he
entered the employment of Draper, Clark & Co., one
of the largest hat, cap, fur, and straw goods houses
in the city of New York, where he remained for three

(167)

MEMORANDA.

years. He then removed to Corning, N. Y., where he
started a boot, shoe and straw goods store. He was
there burned out, and returned to New York City,
where he formed a partnership with William Walker,
in a hat, cap and fur store in Canal Street, but owing
to the hard times and stringency in money matters
generally, they closed out the stock, and he returned
to Piermont, where he was married. Just before the
war he again entered mercantile business in company
of Isaac D. Blauvelt. At the close of the war he
removed to St. Louis, Mo., where he was engaged in
the insurance business until 1888, when he returned
to Piermont, N. Y., where he now resides. Their
church relationship is now with the Dutch Reform.
While they were in St. Louis they were connected with
the Presbyterian Church.

(129)

II. ELIZABETH ATWATER was born April 24,
1827, and died October 25, 1854. She was single.

(130)

III. WALTER VARICK was born February 18,
1829. He married at Leroy, N. Y., June 27, 1861,
Helen Jane Paige, who was born at Salisburg, N. H.,
September 27, 1834. and died at Rochester, N. Y., September 4, 1884. He was a graduate of Hamilton College in the class of 1851. Princeton Theological Seminary, 1856, and ordained to the ministry in 1857. He
was pastor of the Presbyterian church at East Pem-
broke, N. Y., from July, 1857, to January, 1861, and
at Ellicottville, N. Y., from 1861 to 1864 when he
received from the American Tract Society the appointment of district secretary with residence at Rochester,

MEMORANDA.

ASA STONE LEACH

N. Y., which position he held until 1893, when failing health caused him to remove to San Diego, Cal., where he now resides.

(131)

IV. SARAH SAPHRONA was born July 17, 1831. She has been twice married. First, May 1, 1856, to George Henry Curtiss. Second, to William Moores. They reside at Waverly Iowa. She has had one child, now dead.

(132)

V. ASA STONE was born October 22, 1833. He has been married twice, first April 2, 1857, to Martha L. Sherman, who died at Westfield, N. Y., April 9, 1875. Second, February 6, 1878, to Ellen S. Barrett.

Dr. Couch has devoted his life to the study, teaching and practice of medicine. He ranks among the foremost examiners and defenders of Homeopathy in the United States. Dr. Couch has an ancestry noted in the fields of medicine and education, and he inherited in an unusual degree those qualities of mind that mark the patient investigator and man of science. After an academic and classical training in Westfield Academy and Chamberlain Institute he took up the study of medicine under the supervision of two eminent physicians of Vermont. He attended courses of study at both Allopathic and Homeopathic Institutes and was graduated from the Homeopathic Medical College of Pennsylvania in 1855. He immediately entered upon the practice of his profession in association with Professor Gardner of Philadelphia. In the same year his *Alma Mater* appointed him demonstrator of Anatomy, and assistant surgeon. He returned to his native county, in New York, and

MEMORANDA.

opened an office in Fredonia, where he has practiced
for forty years. The esteem in which he is held in his
profession, and in the community in which he lives is
best attested by the positions of trust and honor to
which he has frequently been summoned. He was for
several years vice-president of the Homeopathic Medical Society of the State of New York and for one year
its president.   He was one of the founders of the
Chautauqua County Homeopathic Medical Society,
and of the Homeopathic Medical Society of Western
New York.

In 1877 he was appointed professor of special
pathology and diagnosis in the Hahnemann College
and Hospital in Chicago, where his lectures were
noted for depth of thought, broad knowledge and
painstaking research. The degree of Doctor of Medicine was conferred upon him by the regents of the
University of New York in 1879, and in 1891 the
Homeopathic Society of the State nominated him for
the State Board of Medical Examiners, to which he
was duly elected by the State regents. He was chosen
president of the first meeting of the Board.

In 1894 by Governor Flower and again in 1895 by
Governor Morton Dr. Couch was commissioned one
of the managers of the Collins' Farm Homeopathic
Hospital for the Insane. As a popular lecturer Dr.
Couch enjoys a wide reputation, presenting compli-
cated subjects in a simple intelligible way. He has
lectured before the Buffalo Society of Natural Sciences, and he delivered the opening address before
the World's International Homeopathic Congress held
at Atlantic City in 1891.

Dr. Couch's whole life has been one of unceasing
activity in the practical and theoretical branches of
his profession, and he is today, in consequence, justly

MEMORANDA.

regarded as a complete all-around physician and scientific man.

(133)

VI. HIRAM was born July 18, 1835. He enlisted at Waterloo, Iowa, August 6, 1862, in the 32d Regular Iowa Volunteers, and died in a hospital at Columbus, Ky., June 29, 1863. He was single.

(134)

VII. BRADFORD was born October 21, 1836, and died December 3, 1868. He was single.

(135)

VIII. HENRIETTA was born May 8, 1841. She married, October 24, 1878, C. C. Kenney, who was born August 24, 1853. He is a photographer. They reside at Markato, Minn. Have no children.

(136)

IX. RHODA ELIZABETH was born August 23, 1843. She married, October 14, 1869, John M. Petterson. They reside at St. Peterson, Minn.

(137)

X. MARTHA was born July 15, 1845, and died July 22, 1876. She was single.

(138)

XI. MARY was born July 15, 1845, and died January 1, 1847.

MEMORANDA

Chapter XXII.

(139)

I. ELIZABETH WEBSTER was born March 8,
1834. She has never married. Now resides with her
father at Westfield, N. Y.

(140)

II. ROLLIN LESTER was born May 3, 1836.
He married at Erie, Pa., February 29, 1860, Maria
McNutt, who was born at Erie, Pa., June 6, 1837, and
died at Elmira, N. Y., August 25, 1888. She was a
daughter of William McNutt, who emigrated to Erie
in the forepart of this century and established the first
cabinet shop in that city. Rollin now resides in
Elmira, N. Y.

(141)

III. LAVINNIA SOPHIA was born June 17,
1839. She has been a teacher in female schools for a
number of years in Kentucky and Tennessee. She is
not married. Now teaching a select school for young
ladies at Winchester, Ky.

(142)

IV. JULIA MARY was born July 24, 1849. She
has been a teacher in a school for young ladies in
Tennessee and Kentucky for several years. She is
single, and is now teaching at Maysville, Ky.

MEMORANDA.

Chapter XXIII

Children of Amos M. (61) and Jane (McConnel) Stone.

(143)

I. WILLIAM A. was born at McMinnville, Tenn., November 30, 1838, and died in May, 1863. He moved with his father's family to Texas in 1855. He was a soldier from Texas in the Confederate Army in the 11th Texas Cavalry, Captain Burk's Company. He was killed near Nashville, Tenn. He was a prisoner of war at the time and was accidentally shot by his own men while they were trying to stop the train he was on. He was single.

(144)

II. RICHARD M. was born June 9, 1840, and died September 3, 1840.

(145)

III. EDWARD P. was born at McMinnsville, Tenn., July 30, 1842. He married, July 4, 1877, Kate D. Boyd, who was born at Greenwood, La. He came to Texas in 1855 with his father's family. In 1862 he enlisted in the Confederate Army in Company F., Whitefield's Legion, and was under General Van Dorn. He was engaged in the first, second and third battles at Corrinth, Miss., at Iuka, Miss., and was with Van Dorn December 20, 1862, when he took Holly Springs, Miss., and captured the garrison of fifteen hundred men, commanded by Col. Murphy of the 8th Wis. Reg., and destroyed all the Union munitions of

MEMORANDA.

war, food and forrage. At the same time Gen. Forest got possession of a line of railroad from Jackson, Tenn., and Columbus, Ky., doing much damage to it. This cut Grant off from all communication with the North for more than a week and from rations from regular stores for more than two weeks. It may be of interest to note that this same Colonel Murphy was the officer who two months before had evacuated Iuka on the approach of the Confederate Army. He was in several other engagements. He had a hip dislocated from a fall from his horse while in the service which has made him a cripple for life. He resides at Bagwell, Texas. He is notary public for Red River County, Texas. They have four children, viz.:

1. Itlie May, was born April 12, 1878.

2. Willie E. was born January 16, 1880.

3. Maggie R. was born August 25, 1882, and died July 24, 1890.

4. Emily E. was born January 13, 1884.

(146)

IV. JAMES LESTER was born July 13, 1844, at McMinnville, Tenn. He moved to Texas with his father's family in 1855. He was a soldier in the Confederate Army, from Texas, in Company F, Whitfield's Legion. He died at Dr. Madron's in Arkansas, July 19, 1863, on his way home; he had been discharged from service on account of poor health. He was single.

(147)

V. ALFRED P. was born at McMinnville, Tenn., September 7, 1847, and died at San Antonio, Texas, March 11, 1896. He married July (——) 1869, Mary

MEMORANDA.

Fleming, who was born October 10, 1849. She died at San Antonio, Texas, December 6, 1894. He was a soldier in the Confederate Army from Texas, in Capt. C. B. Sutton's Company. Their service was mostly on the Gulf and in Louisiana. After the war he came home and took charge of his father's estate in company with his brother Amos. They had four children, viz.:

1. Alice was born December 30, 1870. She is a teacher in public schools at San Antonio, Texas. She is a young lady of high mark and held in high esteem by all who know her.

2. Ella was born March 20, 1880.

3. Finis was born November 5, 1881.

4. Lola was born April 7, 1888.

5. Amos was born December 13, 1893, and died May 4. 1895.

Children of Amos M. (61) and Margaret L. (Rogers) Stone.

(148)

I. AMOS M. JR. was born at McMinnville, Tenn., October 15, 1848. He came to Texas with his father's family in 1855. He has been married twice. First, October 2, 1870, to Sadie Hamilton, who died January 7, 1885. They had four children, viz.:

1. Sam M. was born August 21, 1870, he married, January, 1896, Altie Baker. He is a manufacturer of lumber and shingles.

2. Imogene was born February 18, 1873. She married, September 12, 1893, W. R. Moore. They have one child, "Ona" (a son) born November 19, 1894.

MEMORANDA.

3. Willie (a girl) was born November 12, 1875. She is assistant postmaster at Bagwell, Texas.

4. Lura was born October 16, 1878.

Amos M. Jr. married for a second wife Vera Johnson, at Marshall, Texas. She is a woman of great worth, being one of the best educators in Sunday-school and church work. They have no children. Her father was an old resident of Marshall, Texas. He was a Cumberland Presbyterian minister, also a practicing physician. Amos M. Jr. is the postmaster at Bagwell, Texas, where they reside.

(149)

II. CLEORA was born July 11, 1850, at McMinnville. Tenn., and died April 24, 1871, at Clarksville, Texas. She married, in March, 1865, William L. Smith. He is a farmer and resides at Blossom Depot, Texas. They had two children, viz.:

1. Maggie, born September 12, 1868; died, July, 1871.

2. Sam Amos, born April 5, 1871; died, 1871.

(150)

III. FRANK was born July 13, 1852, and died July 14, 1852.

(151)

IV. HENRY R. was born September 14, 1853, and died December 23, 1853.

(152)

V. MARGARET L. was born October 4, 1854, at McMinnville, Tenn. She married, December 23, 1883, J. N. Ellis, who was born March 25, 1849, in Davidson County, Tenn. He was educated at Newburn, Tenn., studied languages in 1877-8 in East Tennessee Univer-

MEMORANDA.

sity, at Knoxville, and was graduated from the National Normal University at Lebanon, Ohio, in the class of 1878. He is now the president of Buffalo Gap College, a school of high grade, under the auspices of the Cumberland Presbyterian Church. They reside at Buffalo Gap. Have two children, viz.:

1. A. Young, born January 22, 1885.

2. Ella May, born May 20, 1890.

(153)

VI. SANNELLA S. was born May 20, 1857. She married in May, 1887, C. M. Gains. They have two children, viz.:

1. Mabel was born (——).

2. Erix was born (——).

They are farmers and reside at Bagwell, Texas.

(154)

VII. ARCHIE ROGERS was born August 20, 1859, at Clarksville, Texas. He married, at Bogata, Texas, October 31, 1882, Izetta Enola Hendrick, a daughter of the Rev. W. R. Hendrick. She was born January 24, 1863, near Bowling Green, Ky. He is a minister of the gospel of the Cumberland Presbyterian Church, was ordained in July, 1890, at Kaufman, Texas, by Order of Bacon Presbytery, Rev. Benjamin Spencer preaching the ordination sermon. He is now pastor of the Cumberland Presbyterian Church at Ballinger, Texas. They have two children, viz.:

1. Luther Amos, born August 20, 1883.

2. Mary Louise, born December 29, 1889.

(155)

VIII. MARY LUCY was born December 15, 1861, and died November 27, 1862.

MEMORANDA

NINTH AND A PART OF TENTH GENERATION.

Chapter XXIV.

Children of Joel (67) and Anna (Stone 86) Stone, all born at Livonia, N. Y.

(156)

I. LUCINDA MARIA was born November 20, 1851, and died June 27, 1870.

(157)

II. MARY ESTELLA was born May 8, 1855, and died January 13, 1871.

(158)

III. JOHN RUSSELL was born April 19, 1858. He married, May 18, 1881, Nellie E. Carey, who was born April 7, 1859, a daughter of Hubbard G. and Mary (Hurlburt) Carey. He was educated in common schools and Canandaigua Academy. He is a farmer, and lumber dealer, and a very successful business man. His residence is one of the handsomest in Livonia, where he resides. He is a Republican in politics, and in religious faith a Presbyterian.

(159)

IV. ELLIS NEWELL was born November 2, 1860. He has been married twice. First, October 23, 1883, at Rochester, N. Y., to Hattie L. Marsh, who

MEMORANDA.

was born May 25, 1858, at Rochester, N. Y., and died
December 17, 1885, at Livonia, N. Y. He married,
second, October 5, 1887, Jennie Short, who was born
January 23, 1858, at Honeoye, N. Y. He was edu-
cated at Genersee Wesleyan Seminary at Lima, N. Y.
They are farmers and reside on the old homestead, at
Livonia, N. Y.

(160)

V. FRANK ELMER was born March 23, 1863.
He married, October 8, 1885, Frances Elberta Fowler,
who was born May 2, 1862. He was educated in common schools and Cornell University. He was for two
years manager of the Conesus Lake Salt Company.
In the winter of 1887-8 he purchased a large tract of
land in Virginia, where they now reside.

MEMORANDA.

Chapter XXV.

(161)

1. FRANCES JANE was born at Orangeville. N. Y., September 23, 1834. She married, April 18, 1852, George J. Hayes, who was born at South Bristol, Ontario County, N. Y., September 26, 1831. Before marriage Mr. Hayes was a druggist at Grand Rapids, Mich., for a time clerk in a dry goods store at Lyons, afterward a bookkeeper at Muskegon, where he remained until marriage. They have been very prosperous and have a fine home. They are members of the church of Christ. Farmers, and reside at Muir, Mich.

(162)

II. ORRIN was born July 21, 1836, at Livonia, N. Y., and died July 24, 1870, at Ionia, Mich. He married, October 3, 1859, at Palo, Mich., Sarah Thompson, who was borne at London, England, April 15, 1839. He was educated in common schools and had a two years course in Olivet College. He was a machinist and received several patents on farm machinery. He was a member of the church of Christ. They had one child.

1. Zoa, born December, 5, 1864, and died September, 10, 1870.

MEMORANDA.

(163)

III. SILAS NORTON was born at Livonia, N. Y., September 10, 1838. He married, July 3, 1859, at Ionia, Mich., Lorana E. Beverly, who was born at South Jackson, Mich., August 4, 1842. She is a daughter of Frances H. and Amy (Page) Beverly who came from Steuben County, New York. He is a farmer, runs a threshing machine in their season, is also a dealer in agricultural implements, in Ionia, Mich., where they reside. They are members of the Church of Christ.

(164)

IV. CHARLES WESTLEY was born at Orangeville, N. Y., September 4, 1840, and died at Ionia, Mich., July 3, 1891. He married, April 18, 1860, at Muir, Mich., Hannah Schell, who was born at Madrid, N. Y., November 20, 1841. They were successful farmers, owning a fine farm near Muir, Mich. They are members of the Church of Christ.

(165)

V. MAHALA ELLEN was born at Orangeville, N. Y., November 23, 1842. She married, at Muir, Mich., February 19, 1863, Jay Olmstead, Jr., who was born at North Plains, Mich., November 29, 1841. He for several years carried on a flour mill and a hotel at Muir, Mich. They now reside on a farm near Muir. They are members of the Church of Christ.

(166)

VI. DARIUS ALLEN was born at Orangeville, N. Y., November 23, 1842. He has been married twice. First, at Lyons, Mich., November 19, 1863, to Augusta Farmen, who was born March 1, 1841, and

MEMORANDA.

died July 1, 1864.   He married the second time, July 18, 1865, Ellen H. Fox, who was born at Lyons, Mich., August 13, 1844.   She is a daughter of Colonel D. M. Fox and Lucinda Fox of Lyons, Mich.   He enlisted in 1860 in Burden's 1st Regiment of Sharp Shooters.   After his discharge he was for a short time a farmer.   In 1864 he became a merchant in Muir, later at Portland.   While at Portland he held the office of township overseer and highway commissioner.   In 1896 he removed to his farm in Ionia, where he now resides.   They have one child.

1. Cora Lorinda, born October 27, 1873.   She married December 12, 1895, Edward R. Averill.   They live at Iron Mountain, Montana, where he is an operator on the Northern Pacific R. R.

(167)

VII. CLARISSA ELPHENE was born March 31, 1852.   She is single and has always been an invalid. She resides with her sister, Mahala E. (165).

MEMORANDA.

Chapter XXVI.

(168)

I. EDWIN was born at Livonia, N. Y., August 3, 1842. He married September 22, 1861, Melinda Rider, who was born in Stark County, Ohio, April 9, 1839. He enlisted in the War of the Rebellion, serving three years. He was discharged, and re-enlisted, becoming a veteran. His service was four years and fifteen days. He has two honorable discharges. They are farmers and reside at Hoytville, Eton County, Mich.

(169)

II. EDWARD O. was born August 3, 1842, and died July 21, 1843.

(170)

III. LIZZIE A. was born December 14, 1844, at Livonia, N. Y. She married, November 17, 1867, John Wurster who was born in Wittinburg, Germany, August 25, 1842. They now reside in Nortonvile, Jefferson County, Kansas.

(171)

IV. WINFIELD was born July 13, 1850, at Livonia, N. Y., and died April 11, 1875, at Pardee, Kan. He married October 17, 1872, Lucetta Birdsell. He was a farmer. She has married a second time and now lives at Salem, Oregon. They had one child, viz.:

1. Walter Elmer was born December 15, 1873. He married Febuary 1, 1896, Allie Stowell, who was born at Walla Walla, Washington, July 21, 1871.

(199)

MEMORANDA.

Chapter XXVII.

(172)

I. FRANK E. was born September 25, 1841, at Lakeville, N. Y. She married, April 23, 1863, George Mortermer Brown, who was born January 13, 1831 at Ontario, N. Y. They reside at Muir Mich.

(173)

II. MARY JOSEPHINE as born November 2, 1844. She married, January 22, 1861, Alexander Willett Case, who was born January 27, 1839, in Livingston County, Mich., and died June 9, 1892, at Ionia, Mich. He was a farmer.

(174)

III. HELEN M. was born November 11, 1847. She married December 25, 1869, Hiram M. Brown, who was born at North Plains, Mich., January 24, 1839. They are farmers and reside at Muir Mich.

(175)

IV. MEDORA, was born March 1, 1850, at Ionia, Mich. She married September 27, 1882, at Muir, Mich.. Charles Frederick Kirby, who was born September 27, 1860, at Oxfordshire, England. They are farmers and reside at Muir Mich. They have had two children, viz. :

I. Frederick B., born May 10, 1889, and died May 10, 1889.

2. Pollie, born August 13, 1891.

(176)

V. GEORGE, was born October 30, 1858, and died October 30, 1858.

MEMORANDA.

Chapter XXVIII.

(177)

I. ORLANDO M., was born May 15, 1846, and died August 12, 1846.

(178)

II. MARY. ROSALIA, was born at Ionia, Mich., June 7, 1848. She married, April 4, 1866, Thomas E. Lippincott, who was born at Batavia, Mich., August 8, 1846, and died at Greenleaf. Kansas, November, 5, 1880. He was a farmer. She resides at Barnes, Kansas.

(179)

III. WILLIAM E. was borne at Ionia, Mich., November 24, 1849. He married, at Effingham, Kan., November 26, 1872, Eunice L. Sherman, who was born at Collins, Erie County, N. Y., May 21, 1849, and died at Barnes, Kansas, January 7, 1895. He is a merchant at Barnes, Kansas. He is a member of the Methodist Episcopal Church.

(180)

IV. JUSTINA E., was born April 21, 1851, and died August 16, 1867.

(181)

V. ALICE A. was born January 28, 1854, at Ionia Mich. She married at Greenleaf, Kansas, October 2, 1872, Edward W. Tate, who was born at

MEMORANDA.

Paolia, Orange County, Ind., February 8 1853.   He has been a farmer, and clerk in a drygoods store.   For ten years has been engaged in general merchandise at Greenleaf, Kansas.   He has held the office of Mayor of Greenleaf and is an elder of the Church of Christ.

(182)

VI. FLORENCE H.   was born at Ionia, Mich., October 13, 1856.   She has been married twice.   First at Greenleaf, Kan., November 18, 1874, to W. E. Bond.   Second, at Greenleaf Kan,. December 25, 1892, to Earl A. Clark.   He is a schoolteacher and farmer.   They reside at Greenleaf, Kansas.

(183)

VII. MIRIAM J. C. was born at Ionia Mich., March 11, 1862.   She married, at Greenleaf, Kansas, July 10, 1881, Floyd C. Allen, who was born in Walworth County, Wis., April 17, 1859.   They are farmers, and reside on the Cherokee Strip.

MEMORANDA.

Chapter XXIX.

(184)

I. GEORGE. WELLS. was born January 16, 1850.
He married, April 23, 1876, Amelia A. Campfield, who
was born in Jefferson County, Wis., March 18, 1856.
They are farmers and fruit growers. He is health
officer and Black Knot Commissioner for Ionia township. They are members of the Church of Christ, of
which he is a deacon. They reside at Muir Mich.

(185)

II. JAMES M. was born November 16, 1851. He
married, June 15, 1878, at Ronald, Mich., Hattie Fea,
who was born at LeRoy, N. Y.. August, 27, 1853
They are farmers and reside at Muir, Mich. He is a
breeder of registered Red Polland cattle and Polland
China swine. He holds the office of Justice of the
Peace. They are members of the Church of Christ,
of which he is one of the elders.

(186)

III. MARY E., was born February 9, 1854, and
died July 29, 1855.

(187)

IV. BABY MAY, was born September 22, 1856,
and died September 22, 1856.

MEMORANDA.

(188)

V. ZACK C., was born September 23, 1865. He married August 3, 1884, Jennie McDunnel. She was born at Attica, Seneca County. Ohio, September 10, 1868. She is a daughter of Henry McDunnel, born in Pennsylvania, December 31. 1820, and died in Ohio, January 14, 1879, (he was a soldier in the Union Army. By occupation a carpenter, cabinet maker and saddler), and Mary E. (Huddleson) McDunnel, who was born in Pennsylvania, January 1. 1826, and died in Ohio, February 11, 1890.

They are farmers and reside at Muir, Mich. They are members of the Church of Christ at North Plans.

MEMORANDA.

Chapter XXX.

Children of Obadiah and Lois (75) (Stone) Tilton.

(189)

I. REUBEN, born August 10, 1842, and died in June, 1843, at Sparta, Noble County, Ind.

(190)

II. ALFRED, born at Sparta, Noble County, Ind., April 10, 1844, and died February 3, 1849, at Orangeville N. Y.

(191)

III. JAMES was born at Sparta, Noble County, Ind., September 3, 1845. He married Violett A. Bump, who was born at Sheldon, N. Y., December 27, 1848, and died at Orangeville, N. Y., April 23, 1875. They had no children. He enlisted September 10, 1864, in Co. G 9th Reg. N. Y. Vols. and remained with the regiment until the close of War. He is a farmer and resides with his mother on the old homestead near Johnsonsburg, N. Y.

(192)

IV. REUBEN JOHN was born August 22, 1847 at Orangeville N. Y. He married, September 27, 1870, Antoinette Royce (a daughter of Hiram Royce) she was born September 5, 1851, at Sheldon, N. Y. He enlisted October 5, 1864, in Co. G 9th Reg. N. Y. Vols. and remained with the regiment until the close of the War. He has held the offices of President of

MEMORANDA.

the Village of Arcade, where he resides, represented his town two terms on the Board of Supervisors, was chairman of the Board of Supervisors of Wyoming County in 1892, and elected Member of Assembly for two terms. He is a merchant. They have no children.

(193)

V. RUSSELL STONE was born at Orangeville, N. Y., April 18, 1840. He married, November 24, 1874, Clara Agnes Barbour, * who was born April 24, 1854. They are farmers and reside near Johnsonsburg, N. Y.

(194)

VI. ALMIRA was born November 10, 1850. She married, November 12, 1869, Dwight S. Camp, who was born at Windsor, Conn., August 30, 1842. They are farmers and reside at Java, N. Y.

(195)

VII. EMMA LUCINDA was born at Orangeville N. Y., November 19, 1852. She married, December 23, 1874, Ira Dixon Calkins, who was born at Sheldon, N. Y., March 11, 1856. They are farmers and reside near Johnsonsburg, N. Y.

---

*She died February 6th, 1897.

MEMORANDA.

GEORGE L. PARKER.

Chapter XXXI

Children of Harvey (76) and Eliza (Lewis) Stone, all born at
Orangeville. N. Y.

(196)

I. ALMIRA ANNETTE was born August 20,
1841. She married, July 5, 1858, George L. Parker,
who was born at Fleming, N. Y., August 19, 1826.
*He was a son of Ira and Anna (Simons) Parker.
When about eighteen years of age he drove team on
the Erie canal for eight months, earning money so
that in the spring of 1845 he went to Troy, N. Y.,
bought an outfit, started on the road afoot peddling
Yankee notions. He soon purchased a horse and
wagon and followed the business of peddling until
1851, when he commenced traveling with Welch &
Drisbach, circus and menagerie having a side show.
The following year he traveled with the famous
showman, P. T. Barnum, and had the celebrated
dwarf "Tom Thumb" with him. Afterward in the
order named he traveled with J. M. June, and with
Ballard & Bailey, who were successors to J. M. June.
Spaulden & Rogers, who introduced the first steam
calliope in America, having forty horses to draw it,
all driven by one man. In the fall of 1857 he gave
up the show business and run a farm for two years.
In the winter of 1860 he commenced business in
Auburn, N. Y., as a merchant. This business he has

---

*He died January 27, 1898.

MEMORANDA.

followed ever since with a degree of success. He is now located at 2319 Main Street, Buffalo, N. Y. They are members of the Bethany Presbyterian Church. They have no children.

(197)

11. MAURICE LEWIS was born August 8, 1843. He married, Febuary 21, 1867 Frances E. Stanley, who was born at Seneca Falls, N. Y., August 26, 1841. She was a daughter of Edwin and Eliza (Chichester) Stanley. Mr. Stanley was a saddler by trade. He was the first warden in the city of Rochester, N. Y. He died at Wyoming, N. Y., at the advanced age of 89 years. Mrs. Stanley now resides with her daughter, Mrs. Ellen Giddings in Batavia, N. Y.

Maurice was educated in common schools and Auburn Academy. In January, 1869, he removed to Benton County, Iowa, and from there in September, 1869, to Wabaunsee County, Kansas, where he continued to live until October, 1875, when he removed to Wamego, Kansas, where he now resides. He is a merchant and has been for many years one of the trustees of the Presbyterian Church, also served as treasurer for the same church. He has held the office of Mayor of the city. He was at one time delegated by the city, together with W. P. Campbell, to interview Charles Francis Adams of Boston, Mass. (who was president of the K. P. R. R.) in regard to some changes that were being made by that railroad company in the city of Wamego.

He was president of the Kansas State Pharmaceutical Association in 1884. He has received a great many Masonic honors and titles. He has taken all of the York rite degrees in Ancient Craft Masonry making him a Knight Templar. He has also taken

MEMORANDA.

the Scotish rite degrees including the thirty-second.
He has passed through the several stations in the
Grand Lodge of the State of Kansas, towit ; "Grand
Senior Deacon" "Grand Junior Warden" "Grand
Senior Warden" "Deputy Grand Master" and was in
Febuary 1898 elected Grand Master, A. F. & A. M.
He served several years as Master of Wamego Lodge
No. 75, A. F. & A. M., also served several years and
is now Most Excellent High Priest of Kaw Valley
Chapter No. 53, R. A. M. He has also served as
"Worthy Patron" of Wamego Chapter No. 76, O.
E. S.

Mr. Stone is a person of Herculean build and
commanding presence. and attracts attention where
he appears. He is a man of high social position and
as a druggist has a large store of varied information.
being one of the best informed pharmacists in his
State, and his opinion on such matters are regarded
by leading druggists throughout the State as of the
highest authoritative value.

(198)

III. TRUMAN LEWIS was born July 1, 1853.
He married, December 2. 1874, Helen Almeda Lewis,
a daughter of Oliver and Louisa (Preston) Lewis, who
now resides at Great Valley, N. Y., and a granddaughter of Jason Lewis who was a brother of Truman Lewis. mentioned in Chapter XIV. (76) Helen
was born at Hinsdale. N. Y., July 18, 1852.

Mr. Stone was educated in common and select
schools, and Warsaw Academy. He has held various
offices of trust, has been the keeper of the Wyoming
County Almshouse and Insane Asylum since 1885.
Has represented the Republican party of his county
in both State and district conventions, he is a trustee of

MEMORANDA

MAURICE L. STONE.

the Presbyterian church at Johnsonsburg, N. Y., is a master mason and member of Wyoming Chapter Royal Arch Masons.

In October, 1897, he received the appointment of Steward at Craig Colony, Sonyea, N. Y., where they now reside. Craig Colony is an institution for the treatment and care of epileptics, it is located at Sonyea (Indian name for Sun Shine) four miles southeast of Mt. Morris, Livingston County, New York. The Colony in some respects is patterned after one at Bielefeld, Germany, although it has more of the mark of American institutions on it, and is probably better built.

MEMORANDA.

Chapter XXXII.

(199)

I. HARVEY BURT was born at North Plains, Mich., August 8, 1855. When quite young he removed with his father to Kansas. He is by occupation a farmer, and now resides at Hydesville, Cal. He is single. He is a Past Noble Grand I. O. O. F.

(200)

II. CLARK MERRILL was born at Muir, Mich., July 4, 1858. He, has been married twice, first November 20, 1876, to Cora Ettie Dickson, who was born at Portland, Mich., March 23 1860, and died September 15, 1887, at Senica, Mo. He married, second, June 17, 1894 at Cleveland, Oklahoma, Lizzie H. Goss, who was born January 30, 1876.

Mr. Sparks is an architect and builder." He was the second settler in Broome County, Oklahoma. He has two children by his firstwife, viz. ;

1. Clayton B. born March 21. 1878.

2. Pearl M. born December 15, 1882.

MEMORANDA.

Chapter XXXIII.

Children and Grandchildren of Hiram and Lucinda (80) (Stone) Smith, all Born at Orangeville, N. Y.

(201)

I. WILLIAM was born January 30, 1854. He married, January 7, 1892, at Eureka, Cal., Mary A. Green, who was born April 1, 1854, at Arlington, Mich. They are farmers and reside at Hydesville, Cal. They have no children.

(202)

II. GEORGE NEWTON was born September 13, 1856. He married, June 23, 1880, Ella Juliet Rose of Wabaunsee, Kansas. She was born at Syracuse, Onandaga County, N. Y., September 22, 1855. They are farmers and reside at Wellers, Jackson County, Oregon. They have had one child, viz.:

1. Eugene, who was born August 19, 1883, and died April 20, 1884.

(203)

III. ALMA was born November 26, 1859. She married at Alma, Kansas, May 1, 1877, Oscar E. Rose, who was born at Syracuse, Onandaga County, N. Y., August 27, 1852. He is a brother of Ella Rose, who married George (202).

They are farmers and reside at Alma, Kansas. They are members of the F. M. Church. They have had seven children, viz. :

MEMORANDA

1. Claude, born June 23, 1878, and died October 7, 1894.

2 Leroy O., born January 12, 1880.

3. Hiram T. born December 11, 1881, and died August 9, 1893.

4. Alma Emma, born October 2, 1883.

5. Jennette Lucinda, born April 24, 1885.

6. Oral Harrison, born November 28, 1887.

7. Paul Gilbert, born June 22, 1894.

Hiram and Lucinda Smith adopted, when quite young, Jennette Amanda Lawton, who was born in Orangeville, N. Y., October 28, 1847. She was a daughter of Rogers Lawton and Harriet Maria (Smith) Lawton, who was a sister of Hiram Smith. Jennette moved to Kansas with her foster father's family in 1869. She married, at Wamego, Kansas, September 25, 1873, William David Perry, who was born November 5, 1839, at Cincinnatus, Cortland County, N. Y. He is a son of Eunice (Young) and Eli Perry.

Mr. Perry moved to Lockport, N. Y., with his father's family when a lad. He was educated in common schools. When twenty-one years of age he bought a boat on the Erie Canal, which he run from Buffalo to New York for three years, when he sold the boat, and went West to Omaha, where he arrived in 1864. He then commenced railroading, afterward became a locomotive engineer on the U. P. R. R., running west from Omaha. He followed this occupation for several years, running over a great many different roads in the West until September 3, 1879, when he went into mercantile business at

MEMORANDA.

Carthage, Mo., where they now reside. Mr. Perry is a member of the Common Council of the city of Carthage. He is also largely interested in mining pursuits near Carthage.

They have had six children viz. :

1. Harriet Eunice was born November 1, 1874. She is a graduate of the Missouri State Normal School in the class of 1894. She is single and now teaching.

2. Willie Edmond was born March 22, 1877. He resides at Carthage Mo. He is interested in mining business.

3. John Lyman was born December 1, 1879, and died young.

4. Jennie Edith was born June 11, 1882. She is a student at the High School in Carthage.

5. Carrie Marie was born June 10, 1885, and died August 25, 1889.

6. Walter Frank was born August 29, 1890.

MEMORANDA.

Chapter XXXIV.

Children and Grandchildren of Edwin (82) and Emma (Crawford)
Stone, all born at Orangeville, N. Y.

(204)

I. JULIA was born March 18, 1863. She was educated in common schools and Warsaw Union School. She taught schools for several terms. She married, September 12, 1883, Charles Marcus Tozier, who was born January 31, 1862, he is a son of Hon. Orange L. Tozier of Sheldon N. Y. They are farmers owning a large tract of land in Vermont. They reside at Pittsfield , Rutland County, Vt.

They have two children viz. :

1. Edwin Stone, born October 13, 1884.
2. Elmer Longmate, born June 26, 1886.

(205)

II. BESSIE LUCY was born October 10, 1872. She married January 14, 1892, George Peter West, who was born at Orangeville, N. Y., December 16, 1869. He owns and runs a portable saw mill. They reside at Varysburg, N. Y. They have one child, viz. :

1. Glen Edwin, born January 30, 1893.

(206)

III. HALLIE was born May 4, 1881. She resides with her parents.

MEMORANDA

Chapter XXXV.

(207)

I. WILSON FRANK born April 20, 1859, and
died July 21, 1862.

(208)

II. EDWIN CECIL was born December 2, 1860.
He married, February 10, 1886, Harriet Tozier, who
was born November 14, 1863. She is a daughter of
Hon. Orange L. Tozier of Sheldon, N. Y. Edwin is
by occupation a cheese maker, and resides at Johnsonsburg, N. Y. They have two children, viz. :
1. Winifred Julia, born December 3, 1886.
2. Frank Tozier, born September 26, 1888.

(209)

III. ELLA MAY was born April 11, 1863. She
married, February 11, 1885, George Hawkins Lewis,
a son of John L. and Lois Lewis. He was born in Orangeville, N. Y., July 4, 1862. He was educated in common schools, and a course of studies in Grand Rapids
University. After which he was employed by
Henry S. Smith of Grand Rapids, Mich., where he
remained until the fall of 1881. In the spring of 1882
he entered into a co-partnership with his father, at
Johnsonsburg, N. Y., and kept a general store. He
finally purchased his father's interest and in 1886

MEMORANDA.

entered into a partnership with Wilson R. Hoy, under the firm name of Hoy and Lewis, in the same business. He subsequently sold his interest to George Hoy, and in 1887 removed to West Nashville, Tenn., where he remained for two years, carrying on a general stock store. On occount of poor health he returned North and accepted a position as head salesman in a drygoods store in Warsaw, N. Y., where they now reside. They are members of the Presbyterian church. He holds the office of Village Clerk. They have had five children, viz. :

1. Frank Glenn, born July 25, 1886, and died September 19, 1886.

2. Vera Mabel. born November 27, 1887.

3. Carrol Hoy, born August 21, 1890.

4. Lucille, Lois, born January 23, 1892. and died August 9, 1892.

5. Raymond McKinley, born February 24, 1896.

(210)

IV. WILSON REUBEN was born October 18, 1865. He married, June 8, 1889, Eva J. Madden. who was born December 9, 1869, a daughter of Edward and Ella (Davis) Madden. She was educated in common schools, Attica Union School and Genesee Wesleyan Seminary, at Lima, N. Y. She was a teacher for a number of terms. Mr. Hoy was educated in common schools and Bryant and Stratton College at Buffalo, N. Y. In 1885 he formed a co-partnership with George H. Lewis in a general stock store at Johnsonsburg, N. Y. Afterward with his father, George Hoy, under the firm name of George Hoy and Son, in 1892, they sold the stock of goods, and purchased a similar stock at Strykersville, N. Y., where the business was

MEMORANDA.

carried on under the same name until the death of George Hoy, when Wilson purchased the balance of the stock. This store he continued to run until 1895, when he sold the goods and rented the store. He removed to Varysburg, N. Y., where he now resides. He then accepted a position as General Agent for the Dayton Computing Scale Company. Mr. Hoy is a member of West Star Lodge No. 413 F. & A. M., also a Royal Arch Mason. They have one child, viz. :

1. Edward Wilson, born September 10, 1892.

(211)

V. HARRIETT LOUISA was born December 29, 1867, and died April 26, 1872.

(212)

VI. ELIZABETH JULIA was born April 14, 1870. She married, October 13, 1892, George Phillip Bauer, who was born September 24, 1864, in Sheldon, N. Y. He is a merchant and resides at Johnsonsburg, N. Y. He is a member of West Star Lodge. No. 413, F. & A. M. They have one child, viz. :

1. Ellis Hoy was born October 31, 1893.

(213)

VII. GEORGE ALONZO was born May 20, 1872. He is single, resides at the homestead at Johnsonsburg, N. Y. He was educated in common schools, Warsaw Union School and Bryant and Stratton College, Buffalo, N. Y. He has charge of a large number of farms belonging to his father's estate. He is also general agent for Western New York for John S. Reese & Co. Fertilizer. He is a member of West Star Lodge No. 413, F. & A. M.

MEMORANDA

(214)

VIII. LUCY ESTELLE was born March 15, 1874. She resides with her mother at Johnsonsburg, N. Y. She was educated in Warsaw Union School. She married January 6, 1898, Howard Bennion of Strykersville, N. Y.

(215)

IX. FRANK ROBERT was born December 15, 1876, and died February 5, 1883.

(216)

X. BLANCH MABEL was born May 10, 1878. She resides with her mother.

MEMORANDA.

Chapter XXXVI.

Children of Alfred (84) and Maria (Carpenter) Stone.

(217)

I. DENCEY MARIA was born October 31, 1847, at
Ronald, Ionia County, Mich. She married, December
25, 1868, George Whitman, who was born at Lima,
Ohio, April 21, 1845, and died at Washington, Gratiot
County, Mich., December 7, 1889. He was a volunteer
soldier in the War of the Rebellion, and was wounded
at Petersburg, June 18, 1864, by being shot through the
right breast and lung. He never had good health afterward. However he cleared up and improved a large
farm. She resides at Ola, Mich.

(218)

II. RHODA ANN was born November 24, 1849.
She married, May 10, 1868, Sylvester Sebring, who was
born March 17, 1846, and died January 10, 1895, at
Crystal Lake, Montcalm County, Mich. He was a
soldier in the War of the Rebellion. He was a farmer, hunter and trapper. She resides at Fishville,
Montcalm County, Mich.

(219)

III. RENA LEVINNIA was born December 25,
1851, at Essex, Mich. She has been married twice,
first June 5, 1868, to Peter Whitman, who was born
February 12, 1847, from whom she was divorced. She
married, second, November 23, 1886, Daniel Curtis,

MEMORANDA.

who was born August 12, 1851, at Scottsville, Monroe County, N. Y. They are farmers and reside at Lyons, Mich.

(220)

IV. AMON was born at Essex, Mich., April 22, 1854. He married, March 14, 1876, at Lyons, Mich., Eliza Dean, who was born at Toronto, Canada, August 18, 1855. He is a farmer, and moves buildings. They reside at Perrinton, Mich. They have no children.

(221)

V. MARY was born at Essex, Mich., February 5, 1856. She married Charles Frederick Webster, who was born March 25, 1854, at Batavia, Genesee County, New York. They reside at Chapin, Saginaw County, Mich.

Children and Grandchildren of Alfred (84) and Lydia Ann
(Lane) Stone.

(222)

VI. LUCY MAY was born September 27, 1861, and died September 17, 1862.

(223)

VII. ELBERT was born October 5, 1863, and died October 15, 1885.

(224)

VIII. CORA was born June 27, 1867. She married May 12, 1893, Lennes Cassady, who was born in Monroe County, Mich., August 23, 1851. He is by

MEMORANDA.

occupation a drayman at Perrinton, where they reside. They have had one child, viz.:

1. Ward, born May 25, 1895, and died August 13, 1895.

(225)

IX. NETTIE was born January 1870 at Essex Clinton County Mich. She married July 17 1887, Charles Winans, who was born November 18, 1865, at Lyons Mich. They reside at Perrinton Mich. They have three children, viz. :

1. Harry Alfred, born August 29, 1889.

2. Pearl, born April 28, 1892.

3. Ethel May, born September 27, 1895.

MEMORANDA.

Chapter XXXVII.

(226)

I. EDGAR D. L. was born January 9, 1855, at Ionia, Ionia County, Mich. He has been married three times, first, January 9, 1879, at Rochester, Mich., to Cora Annetta Terry, who was born at Rochester. Mich., March 11, 1856, and died at Muir, Mich, August 13, 1882. He married, second. October 23, 1883, Mary Laura LaDow, who was born at Johnsonsburg, N. Y., August 30, 1854, and died October 8, 1890, at Muir, Mich. They had one child. viz. :

1. Seth Martin, born September 30. 1890.

He married, for a third wife, at Ionia, Mich., October 28, 1891, Sarah Jane Millard, who was born at Berlin, N. Y., December 10, 1860. They have no children. They are farmers and reside at Muir, Mich.

(227)

II. ELLA was born June 13, 1862, and died September 13, 1880.

MEMORANDA.

Chapter XXXVIII.

(228)

I. ELIZABETH JEWETT, was born June 11, 1846. She married, December 30, 1869, William H. Stanton, who was born at Honesdale, Pa., July 13, 1844. He was educated at Flushing, Long Island. They now reside at Honesdale, Pa. They have had three children, viz. :

1. Harriett Rena, who was born January 5. 1871. She is single.

2. Katharine Niven, was born November 2, 1874. She is single.

3. Mary Waller, was born December 24, 1879, and died August 6, 1880.

(229)

II. MARY STONE, was born October 28, 1858. She married, June 24, 1886, Henry Morris Crowell, who was born at Newark, N. J., June 29, 1853. They reside at Ridgewood, N. J. They have had three children viz. :

1. Charles Waller, was born March 28, 1887, at Newark, N. J.

MEMORANDA.

2. Elizabeth Jewett, was born March 20, 1889, at Newark, N. J.

3. Sarah Weeden, was born July 25, 1890, at Chatham, N. J., and died August 2, 1893.

Chapter XXXIX.

Child and Grandchild of Marcus and Jane Elizabeth (91) (Stone) Sayre.

(230)

1. HENRY NIVEN, was born September 4, 1856. He married, October 25, 1879, Louise Martz. He is connected with the Marcus, Sayre Co., of Newark, N. J., dealers in masons' materials. They have had one child, viz.:

1. Ethel Martz, who was born November 25, 1885, and died June 23, 1888.

MEMORANDA.

Chapter XL.

Children and Grandchildren of Horace Chapman and Charlotte Niven (92) (Stone) Hand.

(231)

I. CHARLES WALLER, was born October 22, 1856, at Honesdale, Pa. He married, at Bloomsburg, Pa., April 26, 1882, Julia Ellmaker Waller, who was born at Bloomsburg, Pa., December 12, 1855. She is a daughter of the Rev. David Jewett Waller (deceased) and Julia Ellmaker of Philadelphia, Pa. Mr. Waller was a Presbyterian minister.

Mr. Hand graduated from Phillips Academy, Andover, Mass., in the class of 1875. He was admitted to the bar at Scranton, Pa., in 1880. He is now the manager of the Davis Oil Company of Brooklyn, N. Y. He is an elder in the Lafayette Avenue Presbyterian Church, Brooklyn, N. Y., where they now reside. In 1897, he was elected treasurer of the Board of Foreign Missions. They have had five children, viz.:

1. Helen Chapman, born January 28, 1883, and died March 23, 1885.
2. Laura Waller, born June 14, 1885.
3. Charolotte Stone, born July 18, 1887.
4. Julia Ellmaker, born April 8, 1890.
5. Dorothy , born May 4, 1895.

(232)

II. ALFRED CHAPMAN, was born at Honesdale, Pa., June 19, 1859, and died at Mansfield, Ohio, March 13, 1892. He married, June 27, 1888, at Mans-

MEMORANDA.

field, Ohio, Sara Lord Avery, who was born at Mansfield, March 18, 1863.

Mr. Hand graduated from Yale College in the class of 1882. He graduated from Union Seminary, May, 1888. The following October he was installed pastor of the Church of the Covenant at Buffalo, N. Y., but on account of failing health he was obliged to resign his pastorate the following winter. He spent the next year and half abroad. They have one child, viz.:

1. Avery Chapman, who was born at Cannes France, April 27, 1889.

(233)

III. HENRY STONE, was born at Honesdale, Pa., February 6, 1865. He married, April 7, 1896, Adelaide Priscilla Coles, of New York City, She was born in New York City, September 2, 1867. She is the daughter of Mr. Barak Gritman Coles, who came from an old Long Island family, the homestead at Glen Cove, Long Island, having been in the family a hundred years or more. Mr. Coles is at present in the provision business in New York city, and his is one of the leading houses in its line in the city. He is a member of the New York Produce Exchange and interested in various other enterprises. Her mother, Mrs. Kate Elizabeth Coles, is of German ancestry, her parents having come to this country in the early part of the present century.

Henry S. was educated at Phillips Academy, Andover and Williston Seminary, East Hampton, Mass. He is associated with his brother Charles (231) in the Davis Oil Company located at 109-113 Ninth Street, Brooklyn, N. Y. He is the treasurer of the company.*

---

*They have one child, Horace Chapman, born Feb. 14, 1898.

MEMORANDA.

Chapter XLI.

Children and Grandchildren of Edwin Fuller and Jennette Scott (93) (Stone) Torrey.

(234)

I. GEORGE NIVEN, was born November 11, 1856, and died April 28, 1860.

(235)

II. JOHN HENRY, was born September 14, 1860. He is in the oil business in Brooklyn, N. Y., where he resides.   He is single.

(236)

III. WILLIAM STONE, was born July 12, 1862. He married, October 14, 1885, Mary M. Hamilton. He is a physician, living in Brooklyn, N. Y.*   They have two children, viz.:

1. Richard Hamilton, born August 5, 1886.
2. Jennette Stone, born June 12, 1893.

(237)

IV. KATHARINE REBECCA, was born June 6, 1866.   She is identified with one of the principal kindergarten schools, in New York City, in which she is a teacher.   She resides at Honesdale, Pa., during the summer.   She is single.†

(238)

V. EDWIN FULLER, JR, was born November 11, 1870, at Honesdale, Pa.   He was educated in a

---

*He died March 4, 1898.

†She married Edward Field Ross, January 5, 1898.   They reside in Philadelphia.

MEMORANDA.

preparatory school at Media, Pa., but did not attend college. After school he was employed as a clerk in the Honesdale National Bank for two years. Afterward as traveling salesman for Thurber, Whyland & Co., of New York. where he remained for five years. He subsequently entered into a co-partnership with O. W. Kennedy, at Clinton, N. Y.. where he now resides. They are general hop merchants. It is the intention of the firm to start in the near future a banking house in connection with the hop business. He married, June 30, 1896, Miss Emma Amelia Kennedy, who was born at Clinton, N. Y., January 6. 1870. She was educated at Houghton Seminary. where she graduated in the class of 1890, and LaSalle Institute at Auborndale, Mass. She has devoted a great deal of time to music and has acquired quite a reputation as a vocalist. She is a daughter of O. W. Kennedy. who was born in Canada. He married Harriet Gruman. He has been in the hop business for the past thirty years and has accumulated quite a large fortune.

Chapter XLII.

Children of George Elliott (102) and Martha (Kays) Stone.

(239)

I. ELIOT KAYS, was born at Scranton. Pa., August 25, 1880. He resides with his parents at Danville, Va.

(240)

II. JAMES, was born at Danville, Va., April 24, 1895.

MEMORANDA.

Chapter XLIII.

(241)

I. ANNA MARY, was born August 23, 1854. She now resides with her mother, Adeline Eliot Stone, on Broad Street, Guilford, Conn., in the house that Timothy (32) speaks of in the letter written to Eber (34) as the house built for Brother Bille. She is single. She has in her possession the deed given by John Leete to her great-great-great grandfather, Caleb (13) July 20, 1714. Also a large collection of family heirlooms, consisting of silverware, china-ware, and household furniture. Among which is a sideboard made of solid mahogany. It was called in its day a Lowdown. It has done service for the Stone family for more than one hundred years, holding the side dishes for innumerable New England dinners. Witnessed family reunions, joys and sorrows. It is a quaint piece of furniture that is duly appreciated by its owner.

(242)

II. WILLIAM LEETE, was born December 13, 1857. He married February 18, 1886, Elizabeth Morrell, of Holmdel, N. J. She was born September 1, 1862. Mr. Stone is a farmer. He resides at the Old Homestead* at the corner of Broad and River streets, Guilford, Conn. He has in his possession the

---

*See Frontispiece.

MEMORANDA.

old deed of the place given by Benjamin Leete, and Rachel, his wife, to Caleb Stone (13) August 30, 1715. This place was the home lot of Governor William Leete, the cellar in which tradition says Governor Leete concealed the regides, Goff and Whaley, still remains, the walls being perfectly sound. Mr. Stone is a genial, companionable man, and takes great pleasure in entertaining his guests which he does in genuine old New England manner. It is very fortunate for the descendants of Caleb (13) that he should be the one to have control of the Old Homestead.   They have four children, viz.:

1. Adeline Eliot, born April 8, 1887.

2. William Morrell, born February 28, 1890.

3. Leverett Camp, born December 10, 1891.

4. Eliot Wyllys, born April 22, 1894.

MEMORANDA.

Chapter XLIV.

(243)

I. IDA JANE, was born June 11, 1867. She married, June 11, 1890, Romanzo VanDeventer. They reside at Aurora, Ill. They have three children, viz.:

1. Emery William, born May 27, 1891.
2. Ira Dodson, born April 17, 1893.
3. Mabel Grace, born January 28, 1896.

(244)

II. BYRON, was born April 13, 1869. He is a teamster in Aurora, Ill. He married February 22, 1898, Miss Lottie M. Rogers.

(245)

III. WILBUR was born July 11, 1872. He is a machine moulder and member of Enterprise band. He is single and resides at Aurora Ill.

(246)

IV. LUCY was born January 31, 1874. She married March 15, 1893, Byron C. Rogers, who was born at Aurora Ill. May 22, 1871. He is a fireman. They have one child viz.:

1. William, born October 16, 1895.

(247)

V. CLARA was born February 18, 1879 and died February 25, 1879.

(248)

VI. LEROY, was born April 17, 1880. He is a silver plate worker.

MEMORANDA.

Chapter XLV.

(249

I. WILLIAM LEANDER. was born November 21, 1858, and died January 4. 1867.

(250)

II. ANNIE T., was born August 15, 1862, and died April 11, 1863.

(251)

III. CARRIE W.,'was born August 15, 1862, and died January 8. 1869.

(252

IV. HARRIETT, was born April 28, 1866. She graduated from Wellesley College, Massachusetts, and is a post graduate of the Chicago University, with the degree of Master of Science. Her specialty is chemistry. She is single. Resides with her mother, at 3352 Indiana Avenue, Chicago, Ill.

(253)

V. ISABELLA, was born October 18, 1868. She is a graduate of Wellesley College, Massachusetts, and a post graduate of Chicago University. Her specialty is physics. She has the title of M. S. P. H. D. She is single and resides with her mother, at 3352 Indiana Avenue, Chicago. Ill.

(254)

VI. NELLIE. was born September 11, 1871, and died July 2, 1872.

MEMORANDA.

Chapter XLVI.

Children and Grandchildren of Henry C. and Harriet Maria (111) (Stone) Dodge.

(255)

I. MEDORA, ELLEN, was born at Kenosha, Wis., January 20, 1856. She married, in October, 1893, Samuel H. Gammon, of Chicago, Ill. He died in Pomona, Cal., October (——), 1894. She has no children. She resides at Ripon, Wis., where she superintends a Kindergarten.

(256)

II. MINNIE MARIA, was born at Kenosha, Wis., June 21, 1858. She married, September 23, 1879, at Chicago, Ill., William M. Goldthwaite, who was born August 5, 1856, at Granby, Mass. He is an electrician and has charge of the city electric light plant, fire alarm, and telephone system of Sanoalito, Cal., where they reside. They have had eight children, viz.:

1. Finley Stone, born Sept., 20, 1880.

2. Lillian Searl, born July 31, 1882, and died May 29, 1892.

3. Henry Adelbert, born November 2, 1883, and died May 4, 1886.

4. Leslie Everett, born July 22, 1885.

5. Nina, born August 22, 1887.

6. Walter Scott, born November 29, 1888

7. Irene, born January 4, 1893.

8. Hartland Dodge, born April 9, 1894.

MEMORANDA.

(257)

III. MARTHA LUELLA, was born at Kenosha, Wis., November 2, 1863. She was educated in Kenosha High School and Oshkosh State Normal School. She has been a teacher since 1881, having taught in Kenosha Co., Eau Claire, Wis., in the public schools. Also the Sheldon and Mulligan schools, in Chicago, Ill. Since 1891 she has been teaching in Eau Clarie, where she now resides. She is a member of the First Baptist Church of Eau Clarie. Se is single.

Chapter XLVII.

Children of Louis B. and Mary Jane (115) (Stone) Bridgman.

(258)

I. WARD A., was born April 20, 1860. He resides at Alcestor, Union County, South Dakota. He is by occupation a photographer.

(259)

II. DELLA M., was born June 4, 1870. She resides at Wakonda, South Dakota. She is a school teacher. She holds a State certificate. She is single.

(260)

III. RAYMOND T., was born March 23, 1872. He is attending college at Yankton, S. D.

Child of Parmenas A. (116) and Harriet (Gibbs) Stone.

(261)

I. ALLAN HIRAM, was born at Ripon, Wis., November 20, 1877. He now resides with his parents at Lansing Mich.

MEMORANDA.

Chapter XLVIII.

Children and Grandchildren of Edward P. (122) and Annis (Larrabee) Stone.

(262)

I. HARLAN D., was born at Alto, Wis., January 28, 1865. He married July 3, 1886, at Zion, Winnebago County, Wis., Fannie Harris, who was born October 4, 1865, at Marquette, Wis. He is a minister of the Methodist Episcopal Church. They reside at Cambelsport, Wis. They have four children, viz.:

1. Ethel Annes, born September 26, 1887.

2. Stella Ruth, born December 29, 1889.

3. Edward Payson, born April 16, 1892.

4. Harlan Asbury, born December 13, 1893.

(263)

II. GRACE S., was born at Alto, Wis., March 25. 1870. She married, September 10, 1890, at Alto Wis., Edward W. Cross, who was born November 4, 1863, at Raymond, Racine County, Wis. They reside at 805 Oakland Avenue, Milwaukee, Wis. They have had three children, viz.:

1. Lucile E., born September 17, 1891.

2. Marian A., born March 21, 1893, died April 7, 1893.

3. Jesse E., born March 19, 1894.

(264)

II. GERTRUDE P., was born at Alto, Wis., March 25, 1870. She married, November 16, 1892, Wallace N. Russel, who was born at Chester, Windsor County, Vt., November 3, 1864. They are engaged in farming and stock raising at Aurelia, Iowa, where they reside. They have one child, viz.:

1. Florence Annis, born October 20, 1893.

MEMORANDA.

Chapter XLIX.

**Child and Grandchildren of Edward A. and Nellie B. (124)
(Stone) Knight.**

(265)

I. HOWARD E., was born November 4, 1864, at Center Creek, Minn. He married, November 3, 1888, Sarah B. Moore, who was born at Fredericktown Ohio, December, 5, 1855. He is a farmer and lumberman. They reside at Viola, Latah County, Idaho. They have had three children, viz.:

    1. Carrie, born July 20, 1889, died August 2, 1889.
    2. Carl, born July 21, 1891.
    3. Ruth, born August 27, 1893.

Children of Orson O. and Nellie B. (124) (Stone) Rundell.

(266)

I. GRACE L., was born at Center Creek, Minn., April 17, 1872, and died December 10, 1886.

(267)

II. EMERSON A., was born at Center Creek. Minn., May 5, 1878. He works in a saw mill at Springfield, Lane County, Oregon. where he resides. He is single.

(268)

III. BERNICE B., was born at Center Creek, Minn., August 21, 1879. She is attending school at the graded school building in Moscow, Idaho.

(269)

IV. ELTON O., was born at Center Creek, Minn., September 26. 1881. He now resides at Princeton, Idaho.

MEMORANDA.

Chapter L.

(270)

I.   ALICE PAIGE. was born at Ellicottville, N. Y., June 20, 1863. She married at Rochester, N. Y., July 27, 1886, William Wallace Young, who was born at St. Catherines, Canada, August 12, 1864.   He is an accountant, a member and deacon of the First Presbyterian Church of San Diego. Cal., where they reside.   Her mother was a graduate of, and afterward a teacher in Ingham University, Leroy, N. Y.   Alice graduated'from the high school in Rochester, N. Y., in 1883. She afterward became a teacher in one of the public schools in Rochester, which position she held until the time of her marriage. They have one child, viz.:

1. Helen Frances, born August 2, 1890.

(271)

II. EDWARD PAIGE. was born September 20, 1866, and died January 6, 1886.   He was single.

MEMORANDA.

Chapter LI.

Children of Asa Stone (132) and Ellen S. (Barrett) Couch.

(272)

I. ELEANOR, was born May 15, 1879.

(273)

II. MEREDITH COLMAN, was born February 5, 1881.

Chapter LII.

Children of John M. and Rhoda E. (136) (Couch) Peterson.

(274)

I. RHODA ELIZABETH, was born July 31, 1875. She is single.

(275)

II. ANNA LOUISA, was born September 28, 1880.

MEMORANDA.

Chapter LIII.

Children and Grandchildren of Rollin Lester (140) and Maria (McNutt)
Stone.

(276)

I. EUDORA, was born May 2, 1861. She married, August 29, 1883, Robert Van Boskirk, who was born December 17, 1852, at Brazil, Clay County, Indiana. He is clerk of the District Court of Iowa County, Iowa, and resides at Marengo, the county seat. They have three children, viz.:

1. Francis, was born at Marengo, Iowa, August 6, 1887.

2. Serrin Stone, was born at Marengo, Iowa, July 7, 1890.

3. Lester, was born at Marengo, Iowa, November 13, 1894.

(277)

II. JESSIE MARIA, was born October 26, 1862. She married, October 1, 1885, William W. Laidlaw, who was born at Troy, Bradford, County, Pa., April 7, 1855. He is general manager of Blight & Warrell's coal office, in Elmira, N. Y. They have two children, viz.:

1. John Lester, born at Elmira, N. Y., August 13, 1887.

2. Frederick Stone, born at Elmira, N. Y., December 18, 1889.

(278)

III. LOTTA, was born at Elmira, December 5, 1867. She remains single, and resides with her father at Elmira, N. Y.

(281)

MEMORANDA.

THE TENTH AND ELEVENTH GENERATIONS.

Chapter LIV.

Children of John Russell (153) and Nellie E. Carey Stone, all born at Livonia, N. Y.

(279)

I. EDITH MAY, was born November 26, 1884, and died December 29, 1884.

(280

II. ALBERT JOEL, was born June 9, 1886.

(281)

III. A son born December 7, 1887, and died December 7, 1887.

(282

IV. MABEL, was born June 18, 1889.

MEMORANDA.

Chapter LV.

Child of Ellis Newell (159) and Hattie (Marsh) Stone.

(283)

I. ELLIS HOWARD, was born at Livonia, N. Y., July 19, 1885.

Child of Ellis Newell (159) and Jennie (Short) Stone.

(284)

I. TRUMAN SHORT, was born at Livonia, N. Y., November 30, 1889.

Chapter LVI.

Children of Frank Elmer (160) and Frances Elburta (Fowler) Stone.

(285)

I. ELMER FOWLER, was born at Livonia, N. Y., January 22, 1887.

(286)

II. MARIA F., was born October 24, 1888.

(287)

III. LUCY E., was born May 2, 1890.

MEMORANDA.

Chapter LVII.

(288)

I. ELIZABETH SYLVAN, was born October 10,
1855.   She married, October 10, 1870, L. N. Olmsted,
of Ionia, who was born January 15, 1852, at North
Plains, Mich.   They have had three children, viz.:

1. George N., was born May 28, 1874, at Ionia,
Mich., and died July 13, 1880.

2. Earnest Pliny, was born at Ionia, Mich., April
9, 1877, and died July 17, 1880.

3. Ernanie May, was born at Ionia, Mich., November 27, 1889.

(289)

II. LILLIAN LEONA MAY, was born July 6,
1865.   She married, January 24, 1888, F. L. Whitney,
who was born in Portage County, Ohio, August 21,
1862.   They have one child, viz.:

1. Ray Hayes, was born March 7, 1894.

MEMORANDA.

Chapter LVIII.

(290)

I. LINNA MAY, was born May 30, 1860. She married. December 18, 1879, Eugene Knapp, who was born July 26, 1846, in Schenectady County, N. Y. He was educated in common schools. He is by trade a carpenter and joiner. Soon after marriage he bought a farm near the village of Muir, Mich., clearing it he has made it a desirable home. They have three children. viz.:

1. Harry, was born March 24, 1881.
2. Allen, was born May 8, 1884.
3. Dedie Inez, was born March 20, 1886.

(291)

II. FRANCIS EARNEST, was born July 18, 1866, and died April 15, 1874.

(292)

III. ORIN, was born in the township of Ionia, County of Ionia, Michigan, September 23, 1872, and from the age of five years attended the country school until the spring of 1886, when he entered the High School at the village of Muir, joining the class of 1890. He also took lessons in music and painting, aside from his school studies, while here. He was a

MEMORANDA.

member of this school for three years. In the fall of
1889 he entered the Ionia High School, where higher
branches were taught. At this school he took a
scientific course embracing two languages, and the
sciences. He graduated from this school in the class
of 1892. He had kept up his lessons on the piano and
pipe organ during the time he attended this school.
He has since been employed by the Ionia City Music
Store. Also has been organist at the State House of
Correction. He is now engaged with the firm of
Simpson & Peer, at Ionia. He is a member of the
Church of Christ at Ionia, and also an active member
of the Christian Endeavor. He was chosen as a
delegate to the National Christion Endeavor Conven-
tion at Boston, Mass., in 1895. He is single.

(293)

IV. JESSIE, was born November 23, 1874. She
married, August 10, 1892, William Crane Peer, who
was born in the township of Berlin, Ionia County,
Mich., July 8, 1869. He was educated in common
schools. In 1885 he entered the drygoods store of
Stone & Carten, at Ionia, where he remained until the
spring of 1892. In the fall of the same year he formed
a co-partnership with Martin E. Simpson, under the
firm of Simpson & Peer. The firm starting with
small capital have increased their trade so that they
now employ six salesmen, and a cashier carrying one
of the first and most complete line of drygoods, silks
and carpets in central Michigan. Mr. and Mrs. Peer
are both active members of the Church of Christ.
They have two children, viz.:

1. Theo born October 20, 1895.

2. Russell Stone, born November 16, 1896.

MEMORANDA.

Chapter LIX.

Children and Grandchildren of Charles Westley (164) and Hannah (Schell) Stone.

(294)

I. MARY MAHALA, was born October 18, 1861. She married, March 23, 1890, William Randall, who was born December 20, 1864, in Genesee County, New York. He received a common school education. They are farmers and reside at Muir, Michigan.

They have two children, viz.:

1. Jennie Stone, born in Genesee County, N. Y., June 11, 1891.

2. Daisy, born at Ionia, Mich., December 13, 1893.

(295)

II. DARIUS GEORGE, was born in Ionia, Mich., May 4, 1863. He married, May 23, 1884, Jennie Jackson of North Plains, Mich., who was born October 15, 1865. He received a common school education. Soon after marriage he took charge of his grandfather's (Darius 69) farm, a part of which he subsequently became owner of. He is a thorough farmer and good business man. They have no children.

(296)

III. CHARLES BEST, was born near Muir, Mich., March 12, 1874. He was educated in common schools, Muir High School, and a course in Poucher College at Ionia, Mich. He is a farmer and since the death of his father he has had charge of the home farm; he is single.

(297)

IV. JUDSON WESTLEY, was born December 4, 1882.

(293)

MEMORANDA.

Chapter LX.

(298)

1. COLONEL JAY, was born July 17, 1864.   He married, July 30, 1885, Lillian May Flower, who was born August 4, 1864.   They now reside at Salem, Oregon.   They have one child viz.:

1. Hazel Margurite, was born in Salem, Oregon, June 28, 1892.

(299)

II. DORUS DARIUS, was born March 20, 1869. He married, August 12, 1891, Mina L. Wolf, who was born September 20, 1872.   They have one child.

1. Zoe Ellen, born August 13, 1892, at Salem, Oregon.

MEMORANDA.

Chapter LXI.

(300)

I. ORILLIE E.. was born October 23, 1865. She married, October 22, 1882, Albert Hulbs. They are members of the Methodist Episcopal Church, and reside at Ozark, Christian County Mo. They are farmers. They have had five children, viz.:

1. Emily Pearl, born March 29, 1884, and died December 5, 1884.

2. Murtle Iva, born September 8, 1888.

3. Twin to Murtle Iva, born September 8, 1888, died September 8, 1888.

4. Son born October 3, 1890, died October 3, 1890.

5. Edwin Lee, born June 20, 1894.

(301)

II. LIZZIE E.. was born February 4, 1868. She married, April 19, 1893, George Wilcox, who was born January 28, 1871. He is a laborer. They reside at Greyling, Crawford County, Mich. They have three children, viz.:

1. Forest, born (————)

2. Bessie May, born (————)

3. Glen Alexander, born January 19, 1895.

(302)

III. MARY F., was born February 16, 1870. She married, June 2, 1892, Charles Hoffman, who was born

MEMORANDA.

March 9, 1870.   They are farmers and reside at Eagle, Clinton County, Mich.   They have no children.

(303)

IV. TRULIA Z., was born December 30, 1872. She married, September 17, 1888, William McDaniels who was born in Elton County, Mich.   They are farmers, and have three children, viz.:

1. Tillie Mandana, born September 9, 1889.

2. Howard Allen, born June 6, 1892.

3. Nora Lena, born March 9, 1894.

(304)

V. CLARA A., was born June 6, 1874.   She married, July 28, 1891, Eddy Collins, who was born July 25, 1870.   They are farmers.   They have one child, viz.:

1. Ruth A., was born December 2, 1894.

(305)

VI. MAUD C., was born April 1, 1876.   She married in 1896, Charles Wooden.

(306)

VII. WILLIE E., was born March 31, 1879.

(307)

VIII. MELINDA E., born November 26, 1881.

MEMORANDA.

Chapter LXII.

(308)

I. JOHN L., was born August 18, 1868, at Ionia,
Mich. He married, at Nortonville, Kansas, January
31, 1889, Mary Kemp, of the same place, who was
born June 10, 1871. He is by occupation a barber.
They have two children, viz. :

1. Edna, was born February 16, 1891.

2. Claude, was born February 4, 1893.

(309)

II. DORA M. was born April 27, 1873, at Pardee,
Kansas. She married, December 31, 1891, Frank Still-
man of Nortonville, Kansas. They are farmers and
reside at Nortonville, Kansas. They have one child,
viz. :

1. Maidia, born January 24, 1893.

(310)

III. DORUS J., was born April 27, 1873, and died
January 24, 1881.

MEMORANDA.

Chapter LXIII.

(311)

I. CARRIE WINIFRED, was born June 9, 1864, and died February 15, 1892. She married, January 11, 1886, W. C. Peck, who was born March 19, 1858. They have two children, viz.:

1. Glenn Dee, born August 9, 1886.

2. Nellie Winifred, born August 9, 1890.

(312)

II. NELLIE MAY, was born June 22, 1866. She married, September 9, 1891, Joseph W. Ellickson, who was born January 3, 1869. They have had an adopted daughter, Winifred, who was born October 23, 1894, and died February 15, 1895.

(313)

III. FREDERIC WARREN, was born May 16, 1869. He married, February 17, 1894, Minnie Hendershot, who was born August 12, 1868. They have one child, viz.:

1. Gladys Genevra, born July 24, 1895.

(314)

IV. LEVI FRANCIS, was born December 30, 1882.

MEMORANDA.

Chapter LXIV.

Children and Grandchildren of A. W. and Mary J. (173) (Burdick) Case, all born at Ionia County, Mich.

(315)

I. JENNIE MEDORA, was born December 11, 1862. She married, January 1, 1882, William Henry Howk, who was born December 31, 1861, at Chesterfield, Mich. They have two children, viz.:

1. Grace Lillian, born September 25, 1884, at North Plains, Mich.

2. Jay Alexander, born March 8, 1893, at North Plains, Mich.

(316)

II. LILLIE MAY, was born August 2, 1865. She married, January 1, 1883, John Irving Hazelett, who was born in Wayne, Steuben County, N. Y., January 7, 1863. They have had two children, viz.:

1. Herman Garfield, born at Ronald, Mich., October 11, 1885.

2. Edith Pearl, born at Ronald, Mich., October 4, 1888.

(317)

III. ARTHUR LEE, was born August 7, 1874. He married, October 27, 1892, Sarah Alida Bridges, who was born September 25, 1874. They have no children.

MEMORANDA.

Chapter LXV.

Child and Grandchild of Hiram M. and Helen M. (174) (Burdick) Brown.

(318)

I. WILLIAM MASON, was born December 7, 1870. He married, August 16. 1893, Floy L. Heydlauff. They have one child, viz.:

1. Judge C. M., born November 5, 1895.

Chapter LXVI.

Children of Thomas E. and Mary R. (178) (Stone) Lippencott.

(319)

I. NELLIE MAY, was born August 5, 1867, and died April 6, 1874.

(320)

II. ALLIE MEDORA, was born August 2. 1872. When seventeen years of age she received a certificate for teaching school, which occupation she followed for several years. She now has a position as stenographer in a bank at Greenleaf. Kansas. She is single.

(321)

III. NELLIE, was born May 9. 1875. and died April 23, 1876.

MEMORANDA.

(322)

IV. FRED, was born March 9, 1877, and died August 8, 1877.

(323)

V. FRANK, was born March 9, 1877, and died August 3, 1877.

(324)

VI. E. EUGENE, was born November 8, 1880, and died May 28, 1882.

Chapter LXVII.

Children of William E. (179) and Eunice L. (Sherman) Stone.

(325)

I. EDNA MAY, was born June 24, 1875, and died October 8, 1880.

(326)

II. LORA BELL, was born June 4, 1880, and died March 1, 1881.

(327)

III. FAY LARVE, was born August 4, 1882, and died July 30, 1884.

(328)

IV. NEVA BERNICE, was born November 26, 1889.

MEMORANDA.

Chapter LXVIII.

Children of Edward W. and Alice A. (181) (Stone) Tate, all born at
Greenleaf, Kansas.

(329)

I. CLAUDE EDWARD, was born October 23, 1881.

(330)

II. LESSIE, was born October 17, 1885, and
died same date.

(331)

III. ARTIE LEE, was born August 23, 1887, and
died August 26, 1887.

(332)

IV. NINA ALICE (adopted) September 16, 1887,
was born June 23, 1887.

Chapter LXIX.

Children of William E. and Florence H. (182) (Stone) Bond, all born
at Greenleaf, Kansas.

(333)

I. CARL, was born August 21, 1875. He is single.

(334)

II. BERT was born March 22, 1878.

(335)

III. LILLY, was born September 12, 1884, and
died August 13, 1885.

(336)

IV. ERNEST, was born August 11, 1886.

MEMORANDA.

Chapter LXX.

Children of Floyd C. and Miriam Iulia C. (183) (Stone) Allen.

(337)

I. MABEL CLAIRE, was born August 7, 1882.

(338)

II. FLOYD GUY, was born October 29, 1884.

(339)

III. JOHN ELMER, was born March 4, 1888.

(340)

IV. HERSCHEL DARIUS, was born September 18, 1891

(341)

V. LETTIE RUTH, was born February 23, 1895.

Chapter LXXI.

Children of George W. (184) and Amelia A. (Campfield) Chase, all born at Ionia, Mich.

(342)

I. BERTHA E., was born June 11, 1878.

(343)

II. GEORGIA Z., was born June 1, 1882.

MEMORANDA.

(344)

III. WILLIAM W., was born October 28, 1883.

(345)

IV. INEZ L., was born February 4, 1886.

(346)

V. JAMES ORIN, was born July 30, 1887.

(347)

VI. EVA A., was born September 16, 1888.

Chapter LXXII.

Children of James M. (185) and Hattie (Fea) Chase, all born at
Ionia, Mich.

(348)

I. JOHN B., was born January 14, 1880.

(349)

II. MYRTA A, was born October 23, 1881.

(350)

III. ERNEST EDWARD, was born February 3,
1892.

(351)

IV. FEA, was born February 3, 1892.

MEMORANDA.

Chapter LXXIII.

Children of Zack C. (188) and Jennie (McDunnell) Chase, all born
at Muir, Mich.

(352)

I. SARAH E., was born August 22, 1885.

(353)

II. JOSEPH P., was born December 17, 1886.

(354)

III. THERESA E., was born March 24, 1888.

(355)

IV. ALEDAH G., was born June 21, 1894.

Chapter LXXIV.

Children of Russell Stone (193) and Clara A. (Barbour) Tilton, all
born at Johnsonsburg, N. Y.

(356)

I. FRED REUBEN, was born August 30, 1876,
and died February 15, 1878.

(357)

II. EUGENE RUSSELL, was born April 1, 1880.

(358)

III. FRANK EVERETT, was born October 17,
1881.

MEMORANDA.

Chapter LXXV.

Children of Dwight S. and Almira (194) (Tilton) Camp, all born near Johnsonsburg, N. Y.

(359)

I. HATTIE L., was born April 22, 1871. She is single.

(360)

II. MARY, was born May 17, 1873. She is single.

(361)

III. B. ESTELLA, was born March 20, 1875. She married, September 12, 1895, Frank H. Stevens, who was born April 18, 1869.

(362)

IV. SUSIE, was born August 2, 1876. She is single.

(363)

V. GEORGE D., was born January 13, 1879

(364)

VI. NELLIE, was born November 14, 1880.

(365)

VII. CLARA B., was born January 21, 1883, and died September 4, 1883.

(366)

VIII. CHARLES T., was born November 26, 1886.

(367)

IX. LELIA M., was born October 11, 1891.

MEMORANDA.

Chapter LXXVI.

(368)

I. GERTIE MAY, was born January 29, 1877. She married, December 20, 1894, George E. Reynolds, who was born at Hinsdale, Cattaraugus County, N. Y., July 3, 1874. He is a clerk in Arcade, N. Y., where they reside. They have one child, viz:

1. Gladys Maybel, born October 25, 1895.

(369)

II. LEON OBADIAH, was born May 21, 1883.

(370)

III. NELLIE ARTHUSIA, was born October 11, 1887, and died (——) 1888.

(371)

IV. REUBEN ODELL, was born June 17, 1892, and died March 24, 1893.

MEMORANDA.

Chapter LXXVII.

Children of Maurice L. (197) and Frances E. (Stanley) Stone.

(372)

I. FRANK MAURICE, was born in Orangeville, Wyoming County, N. Y., November 24, 1867, and died in Wabanusee, Kansas, February 13, 1871.

(373)

II. MARY ELIZA, was born at Wabanusee, Kansas, February 1, 1872. She attended school at Wamego Union School and at the Rockford, Ill. Female Seminary in 1887-88, where she received a classical education. She is a fine musician. She is single and resides with her parents at Wamego, Kan.

Chapter LXXVIII.

Child of Truman Lewis (198) and Helen A. (Lewis) Stone.

(374)

I. THEO E. LEWIS, was born March 10, 1876. She graduated from the Varysburg school, in the first class that ever held commencement exercises in that school in 1892. After a four year course in Houghton Seminary, a boarding school of high grade for young ladies at Clinton, N. Y. She graduated in the class of 1896. She was vice-president of her class and was chosen to make the responsive address to the Allumni at the commencement exercises. In September, 1896, she entered the New England Conservatory of Music at Boston, Mass., where she is taking a classical course in pianoforte, organ, theory, harmony, and voice culture.

MEMORANDA.

Chapter LXXIX.

(375)

II. MINNIE, was born July 16, 1869. She is single.

(376)

II. CARRIE, was born July 3, 1871. She is single.

(377)

III. PEARLY, was born August 12, 1873. She married Arthur Morse, who was born October 24, 1869. They reside at Washington, Gratiot County, Mich. They have one child, viz.:

1. Jessie, was born December 22, 1891.

(378)

IV. CLAUD, was born August 21, 1878.

(379)

V. ROY, was born March 2, 1882.

(380)

VI. VINA, was born July 18, 1884.

(381)

VII. LYDIA, was born August 1, 1868.

MEMORANDA.

Chapter LXXX.

Children and Grandchildren of Sylvester and Rhoda Ann (218) (Stone) Sebring.

(382)

I. ALFRED, was born June 11, 1869. He is single.

(383)

II. JENNIE, was born at Essex, Clinton County, Mich., August 2, 1871. She married, July 1, 1888, John Folman, who was born February 11, 1864, in Germany. They reside at Perrinton, Mich. They have had two children, viz.:

1. John Sylvester, born December 27, 1889, and died August 21, 1890.

2. Vernie, was born August 30, 1892.

(384)

III. ANOLA, was born July 21, 1873, and died September 8, 1873.

(385)

IV. ERNEST, was born March 9, 1884.

(386)

V. FRANK, was born September 14, 1890.

MEMORANDA.

Chapter LXXXI.

Children and Grandchild of Peter and Rena L. (259) (Stone) Whitman.

(387)

1. JOHN G., was born November 23, 1869, at Greenbush, Clinton County, Mich. He married, February 22, 1891, at Saginaw, Mich., Jennie Patterson. They reside at Fork Mecosta, Mich. They have no children.

(388)

II. ELSIE, was born December 25, 1871, at Greenbush, Clinton County, Mich. She married, January 25, 1888, at Mount Pleasant, Isabell County, Mich., Butler Lott. They reside at St. Louis, Gratiot County, Mich. They have one child, viz.:

1. Reuben Valentine, was born February 14, 1894.

(389)

III. NELLIE, was born May 9, 1874.

Chapter LXXXII.

Children of Charles F. and Mary (221) (Stone) Webster.

(390)

I. MARY, was born March 9, 1879.

(391)

II. MYRTIE, was born October 20, 1881.

(392)

III. LYDIA, was born February 20, 1883.

MEMORANDA.

APPENDIX.

EXPLANATION.

The numbers in the center of the page refer to margin numbers on left hand. The names following the center number are the children of the person referred to. The Roman numbers indicate the number of children in each family.

Genealogy of William Stone, the Brother of John [2] for Several Generations.

It may be of interest to add this brief genealogy as Lois Stone, the wife of Russell (30) is a descendent of William, the immigrant, who came to America in 1639 together with his brother John (2,) William Leete and others.

1. WILLIAM STONE, a brother of John Stone, the emigrant, came to Guilford, Conn., with his wife Hannah in 1639 in the first Guilford, Company. His first wife died in Guilford, and in 1659, he married second, Mary Hughes. William was a farmer and kept an inn at East Guilford (now called Madison) he had by his first wife three children, viz.:

(1)

2. I. William, was born in 1642, he was married twice, first to Hannah Wolfe, a daughter of Edward Wolfe of Lynn, who died March 28, 1712. He married, second, Mary (——), who died July 6, 1732.

MEMORANDA.

3. II. Hannah, was born in 1644. She married, in 1664, John Norton, who was born in 1628, and died March 5, 1704.

4. III. Beneajah, was born in 1649. He married Hester Kirby.

(2)

5. I. WILLIAM, son of William (2), was born March 22, 1676. He married, October 28, 1701, Sarah Hatch of Guilford, who was born in 1681, and died November 26, 1751. He died September 21, 1753.

6. II. Hannah, was born July 27, 1678. She married William Leete.

7. III. Daniel, was born July 27, 1680. He married, January 21, 1708, Elizabeth Talmadge. He died in 1713.

8. IV. Elizabeth, was born November 20, 1682. She married, Joseph Bishop. She died May 16, 1767.

9. V. Josiah, was born May 22, 1685. He married Temperance Osborne, June 29, 1705.

10. VI. Stephen, was born March 1, 1690, and died December 24, 1753. He married Elizabeth Leman, a daughter of Christopher Leman and Esther Barnett, who was born October 9, 1691.

(5)

11. I. Ezra, was born June 12, 1703, and died July 18, 1703.

12. II. JEHIAL, son of William (5) was born November 11, 1705, and died October 18, 1780. He was married twice, first to Sarah (——), who died Novem-

MEMORANDA.

ber 8, 1728. He married, second, June 10, 1730, Ruth White, who was born September 28, 1703.

13. III. Thankfull, was born June 10, 1708, d. y.

14. IV. Thankfull, was born June 25, 1710, and died August 13, 1729. She married Daniel Hubbard.

15. V. Daniel, was born August 29, 1711, and died December 23, 1782. He married Leah Norton.

16. VI. Reliance, was born September 24, 1712, and died April 1, 1757. She married Abraham Braley.

17. VII. Zeroiah, was born July 14, 1715, and died January 8, 1769. She married John Hubbard.

18. VIII. Ezra, was born July 14, 1717, and died March 20, 1798. He married Elizabeth Osborne.

19. IX. Beata, was born June 26, 1723, and died July 27, 1727.

(12)

20. I. THOMAS, was born March 16, 1731. He married January 28, 1772, Leah Norton, who was born in 1735. She was a daughter of Daniel and Sarah (Bradley) Norton, and granddaughter of John, who was a grandson of Thomas Norton. Her brother, Daniel married Sarah 2/.

21. II. Sarah, was born September 2, 1732. She married Daniel Norton a brother of Leah Norton 20, he (Daniel) was born in 1733, and died May 25, 1813. Their daughter, Lucy, born March 18, 1755, and died March 17, 1830, at Greenville, N. Y. Married, October 1, 1777, David Morse, who was the father of Simeon Morse of Orangeville, N. Y., born October 4, 1781, at Guilford, Conn., and died at Orangeville, N. Y., July 27, 1867. He (Simeon) was the father of James Harvey, who was born June 22, 1802, at Greenville, N. Y., and died May 1, 1878, at Orleans, Mich. He (James Harvey) was the father of Catharine, born July

MEMORANDA.

4, 1831, at Orangeville, N. Y. She married, July 3, 1849, Prof. Horace Briggs, now of Buffalo.

22. III. Elisha, was born August 16, 1734. He married Thankfull Hotchkiss.

23. IV. Ruth, was born March 23, 1736. She married Daniel Clark.

24. V. Noah, was born June 23, 1738.

25. VI. William, was born January 23, 1740.

26. VII. Aaron, was born October 25, 1741. He married Lois Dudley.

27. VIII. Isaac, was born February 25, 1743. He married Parthena Dudley.

28. IX. John, was born September 2, 1745, d. y.

29. X. Noah, was born in 1746.

30. XI. John, was born in 1749. He married Mary Parmelee.

(20)

31. I. Zeruah, was born April 30, 1757. She married, Edman Shelley.

32. II. LOIS, was born April 26, 1760. She married Russell Stone 30 (see page 69). Thus after six generations the descendants of John Stone (2) and William his brother intermarry.

33. III. Leah, married James Bradley.

34. IV. Thomas, was born September 27, 1755. He married Mary Stone.

35. V. Jehial, was born (——). He married Ruth Norton. He settled in the Black River country, N. Y.

36. VI. Parnell, married James Bradley.

INDEX.

www.ingramcontent.com/pod-product-compliance
Lightning Source LLC
Chambersburg PA
CBHW021539110726

47902CB00004B/945